A STORM OF PLEASURE

A STORM OF PLEASURE

TERRI BRISBIN

B
BRAVA

KENSINGTON PUBLISHING CORP.
www.kensingtonbooks.com

BRAVA BOOKS are published by

Kensington Publishing Corp.
119 West 40th Street
New York, NY 10018

All Kensington titles, imprints and distributed lines are available at special quantity discounts for bulk purchases for sales promotion, premiums, fund-raising, educational or institutional use.

Special book excerpts or customized printings can also be created to fit specific needs. For details, write or phone the office of the Kensington Special Sales Manager: Kensington Publishing Corp., 119 West 40th Street, New York, NY 10018, Attn. Special Sales Department. Phone: 1-800-221-2647.

Brava and the B logo are Reg. U.S. Pat. & TM Off.

ISBN-13: 978-0-7582-3518-3
ISBN-10: 0-7582-3518-6

First Kensington Trade Paperback Printing: October 2010

10 9 8 7 6 5 4 3 2 1

Printed in the United States of America

Prologue

Gairsay Island, Earldom of Orkney
April 1098 AD

The sun had barely broken over the morning's horizon when Earl Magnus's men rode into the village. It took but moments to realize their arrival had little to do with honoring her father for his work on the earl's behalf. Indeed, their swords brandished against the gray and cloudy sky and their shouts and demands for her father and brother to present themselves told Katla Svensdottir the seriousness of this dawn visit.

Wrapping her cloak around her shoulders and covering her hair with a scarf, Katla crept outside and approached the gathering from the side. Using several smaller outbuildings as cover for her movements, she made her way around to a place where she could hear and see without being seen herself. She caught her brother Kali's eye as he was dragged forward to stand next to their father. With a narrowing of his gaze, Kali warned her to stay away.

Sven Rognvaldson was a bear of a man, and though his hair might carry the gray of age, his broad shoulders were still strong and muscled from years of hard labor and fighting. His raised voice could still send chills down her spine with the essence of command it carried.

And one thing she knew with certainty about her father: he did not allow any question or insult to his honor to go unmarked. Many men had fallen beneath her father's sword for questioning his actions or his intentions. Katla remained pressed against the storage barn out of sight, but not out of hearing distance.

"By what right do you dare this?" Sven's voice nearly made the wall behind her shake with his anger.

"In the name of Earl Magnus," the man replied loudly but not as loudly as her father had yelled. "He demands your presence in Birsay on the morrow to answer to the charges against you."

Katla could not stop herself from stepping closer to the commotion then. No one would dare challenge her father without permission from the earl; to gain it, the matter must be of the utmost importance. The earl did not meddle in his chiefs' personal business or in the way they handled those under their command or on their lands. If no one encroached on lands or cattle or slaves belonging to another, the earl concentrated on other matters that would line his pockets, fill his byres, or increase his standing in the eyes of the king.

A few of those watching turned to look at her as she took one step, then another forward, visible but not in the center of the trouble. Not yet. She waited for her father to gain more information from the earl's man—she knew him well enough to know he was waiting to weigh his choices. Escape? Fight? Surrender? Katla read the expressions on his face as they passed through his thoughts. Only surrender was not truly a choice he would make and the soldiers seemed to know that.

To a one, their stances tightened and the air filled with tension as her father took a step toward the earl's man, growling a question at him, just loud enough for the two of them to hear. Magnus's man's face reddened and he rose to his full height, shoulders squared and legs spread.

A fighting stance she recognized at once, as did everyone else watching the scene unfold.

Her father drew his sword before anyone could say a word, but another of the earl's men anticipated his action and thrust his sword first—into her father's chest! Chaos erupted in that moment and several minutes passed before order returned to the yard and to her father's people. Katla pushed her way past two of the soldiers to her father's side as he lay on the cold ground. Blood poured from the gaping wound in his chest, and she knew his death was close at hand. Of all the ways she had ever considered he would meet his end, this death was not one of them. Shock threatened to overwhelm her until she felt her father's hand tighten around her wrist. Leaning down, she searched his face as she heard her brother arguing nearby.

"Girl," her father rasped out. "Katla."

She watched as he struggled to hold on to whatever moments of life yet remained. "Father?"

"Save him," he ordered with far more vigor than she would have thought possible. "Do what you need to do, but save him."

"How?" she asked in a whisper. "Tell me how!"

Kali was younger than she by two years and though he would inherit most of their father's lands and power when the time came, he was still a brash and sometimes foolish young man. In spite of having different mothers, they were closer than most siblings were and Kali accepted her counsel when the words of others went ignored.

"You must find a way," he uttered on a strangled breath. The gurgling sounds from his throat and chest increased until he could speak no more. Katla could only watch in horror as he exhaled his last breath and then moved no more.

The air around her seemed to stop and become silent as she shrugged off the hand of someone pulling roughly on her shoulder. Only the sound of her own breaths and the beat of her heart echoed in the growing silence. Her ears buzzed with a strangeness she'd not experienced before, and she glanced around to see everyone staring at her and the man on the ground. Turning back to her father, she noticed the blood seeping into the ground under her knees and that his grasp of her wrist had slackened, allowing her to move away.

Save him, he'd ordered.

Katla looked over at Kali, pale faced and shocked, knowing he was uncertain whether he should follow his father into death. She struggled to her feet, searching for words that would help. She still knew not the reason for the earl's summons or why her father would attack in such a way, without enough of his own men to improve his odds of success.

Save him.

The words echoed through her mind as she crossed the short space between her and the man who'd killed her father, the man who now controlled the fate of all those present.

Save him.

"The earl ordered such an act?" she asked of the one in command. "Did he send you to Sven Rognvaldson?" Straightening to her full height, she glared at him as only Sven's daughter could, a look she'd mastered while yet a child and one that everyone exclaimed was the exact likeness of her father's glare.

"I am Harald Erlendson, retainer to Earl Magnus and sent to bring the traitor Sven Rognvaldson to face the earl's justice." She gasped at his words, both from the insult and from the possibility of such a thing. "He brought on his own death. . . ."

"It is no wonder he drew his sword at your words," she said coldly, spitting on the ground. "No one can make an accusation like that and not expect my father to . . ."

Even as she began to say the words, the realization struck her. They had known her father would strike out, and it had given them a chance to kill him. They'd wanted him to attack and he had, giving them the excuse they needed to execute him without allowing him to defend his honor.

"And my brother? Why did you summon him?" Katla's blood chilled and she prayed that her brother would give them no reason to strike him down in the same way.

"He is also called traitor by the earl," the man said loudly enough for everyone to hear.

The shocked gasps and cries spread through the growing crowd, which Katla suspected was the reason he'd announced it as he had. All this could have been handled differently, but doing it in front of everyone made the insult worse. Suddenly, her brother broke free from those who held him and Katla knew he would go for a weapon. She ran to him and placed herself before him.

"Nay, Kali," she warned. "It is a trap. Do not resist them." For once Kali did not put his vanity before his sense, and he stopped fighting the men. "Do not give them a reason to kill you as they have killed our father," she whispered while the soldiers regained their hold on him.

Katla turned back to face Harald Erlendson. Only bold and public action would forestall Kali's execution, for she did not doubt that his death was their true aim.

"Have you seen the proof that would mark my brother traitor, Harald Erlendson? Do those pointing the finger at my father and brother put their name to such accusations? Who has spoken to the earl?"

From the way his face reddened and his gaze hardened,

Katla knew she had touched on some element this man wanted hidden from view. She pressed on. "If you are a man of honor, you will not allow this, Harald Erlendson." She crossed her arms and met his eyes, waiting for him to take or refuse her challenge. She was only a woman, so he could ignore her and not lose status, but her unanswered questions would spread. "Will you make certain that my brother lives to face the earl's justice?"

Those watching waited for the earl's man to reply, but Katla did not. Stepping closer to him, she lowered her voice and spoke only to him.

"I would be indebted to you, Harald Erlendson. If you could see my brother safely to the earl and make certain that proof decides his fate." She paused and met his gaze with her own. "I would be in debt to you."

Though never called on to use her womanly figure or to flirt as many young women her age did around men, she had practiced such skills on occasion to draw the gaze of young Bjarni Einarson. Her father would have punished her if he'd known of such things, but now she was glad she'd learn to pitch her voice lower and to soften her sometimes stubborn expression by gazing up through the lashes of her eyes. She did it now, understanding that she was offering more than simply her thanks to this powerful man who held her brother's life, and her own, in his hands.

She noticed the flush in his ruddy face and the glimmer of lust in his dark eyes when they met hers. Her body trembled then, realizing what she was promising in exchange for her brother's safety. Straightening her shoulders, she nodded in silent acceptance of the cost. If her father lived, this man would not be high enough in status to approach him with an offer of marriage, but everything had changed in that chaotic moment. Now, the proud daughter of one of the mightiest chiefs in Orkney had bartered her body and her virtue for the promise, nay, the hope of help.

Harald barked out orders to his men, and less than an hour later Katla found herself riding out of their village, captive as much as her brother and with as little control over her fate as he.

Her father had demanded that she do whatever was necessary to save her brother, and she would do all in her power to succeed—no matter the cost.

Chapter One

Northwestern Coast, the Norse Southerlands
(Scotland)
Three months later

Gavin took a deep breath and released it.

Again and again, he repeated it, fighting the vice-like pain that pierced his head. He fought the urge to drink the foul brew brought to him by the latest healer. And all the while, he tried to block out the growing noise around him.

The dark of the moon was not even here, and already he recognized that the pain would soon be unbearable. And the damned noises in his head assaulted him more fiercely with each passing day!

Another breath. In and out. And again.

No relief. Only growing pain and thunderous noise filling his head until he wanted to bash his brains against the cliff side and end it all. Reaching for the bitter concoction, Gavin decided to give in to the weakness and seek the solace offered in its swirling depths. He tugged the stopper from the bottle and swallowed its contents mouthful by mouthful until the bottle was empty.

The wizened old man squinted as Gavin finished the brew, saying nothing, only watching as though something terrible was about to happen. The herbal drink rolled roughly in his belly, and for a moment or two, Gavin thought he would vomit it up, but soon it settled.

"And now?" the old man asked, stepping closer and sniffing the air as though there was some sign of change evident in his body's odor.

Even the softly spoken words jarred him, adding to the din and to his pain. The never-ceasing pain of these last months.

"Argh," he cried out, throwing the bottle against the cave wall. "It is not working at all!" Gavin held his head in his hands, pressing against his skull, trying to ease the pain somehow.

Somehow.

"Get out!" he yelled, chasing the old man to the opening of the cave, where the sea now lapped against the walls. "Get out!"

Gavin sank to his knees, grimacing and clenching his teeth against the torment as the healer scrambled past him. He could not salvage an ounce of sympathy for the man's uneven gait or difficulty avoiding the incoming waves of frigid ocean water. The pain tore away all vestiges of compassion or caring. As his servant tugged the man into a small boat and began to sail him along the narrow passage of water that led to his cave, Gavin collapsed on the cold rock floor and prayed that the drug would work.

Then he felt it. Not a cessation of the pain, but a momentary lapse in the constant skull-shattering noise that vibrated through his head all the time.

Just a moment, but the relief was sheer bliss.

He heard . . . nothing.

Nothing in his thoughts. Only the sounds of the crashing

waves and the river that poured through the opening overhead as it rushed to join with the sea.

Nothing.

But just as quickly as it happened, the silence ended and the throbbing clamor pulsed back to its original level. Gavin struggled to his feet, pushed the hair out of his eyes, and searched for the cause of the interruption.

His servant was gone, taking the healer back to his village farther west along the coast. No one else ever remained here with him, not even the women sent by the earl to keep him satisfied as the time for his revelations of truth approached. His only companion was the clatter—relentless, ever-growing, maddening noise—and the pain that accompanied it.

Gavin stumbled then, landing on the stone floor. His limbs felt heavy and his eyes weighted closed. Ah, the healer's concoction did have some effects after all. Rolling to his knees, he crawled toward the drier part of the cave, seeking some place to lie while the brew did its work.

As the drug drew him into some stupor, he felt the silence once more. This time, he could feel it coming from a specific direction. He laughed harshly at such nonsense. How did silence come from a place? Gavin forced his eyelids apart and stared up where the silence seemed strongest.

It was gone as quickly as it had happened.

Closing his eyes, he realized that the sensations rushing through him from this brew were not unpleasant after all. It did not remove the clamor or the pain, but it eased his body in a pleasurable way. He might have to have Haakon bring the healer back after all. Gavin sank deeper into the lethargy until his body began to react as it did when the revelations approached.

Lust filled him, swirling in his veins and in his skin and in his cock until it stood ready. He tried to fall more deeply under the control of the brew, tried to relax and ignore the growing need that heated his blood, but like the relentless noise in his thoughts, it could not be ignored. Since it would be hours before Haakon returned and since Haakon was the only person permitted to bring women here to his sanctuary, there would be no way to quench this latest fire in his blood.

Well, there was a way, but it was never as satisfying as finding release deep inside the tightness of a woman.

Gavin threw his arm over his eyes and breathed in and out, trying to block the lust and need in his body and the sounds in his head. Just as he reached down to ease himself, he heard it. Not another moment of silence, but the soft sounds of footsteps near him.

It should not surprise him that the scent his body gave off had called a local woman to him. It had happened before. No doubt, it would happen again. It *had* happened again. Whatever controlled the power within him to hear the truth and to reveal the truth hidden in the thoughts and hearts of others made certain that his growing need for sex was filled.

It seemed not to matter if he wanted a woman or if he did not; his body threw out the call and women answered.

Now, in spite of the herbal brew dulling his senses, it had done so again.

Gavin moved his arm away and forced his eyes open to see what his visitor looked like . . . and he lost his breath.

An angel or a Valkyrie, he could not decide, stood hovering above him. Curling locks of long blond hair flowed over her shoulders to her hips, and eyes of a glowing dark blue were the first things he noticed about her.

With both the drugs and the lust flowing through his veins, he watched as the light pouring into the cave outlined her womanly figure. Full breasts pressed against the costly cloth of her tunic, and he could not miss the hips and legs that promised him a soft ride. But he found himself lost in the appealing fullness of her lips.

She stood close enough that he could touch her, and he struggled to reach out to her. Gavin managed to clasp her ankle and then slid his hand along the well-worn leather of her boot until he touched her skin. The gasp that filled the cave made him smile.

"Valkyrie, am I to die?" he whispered, knowing the true mission of those fabled servants to the old god Odin. Death would be the ultimate release—from the pain and the curse of his powers. "Am I for Valhalla?"

Gavin knew that the beliefs of old were gone, but this woman stood as proud as one of the legendary choosers of the slain would. She shook her head in reply and he watched as the action caused her hair to swirl around her like a halo. He slid his hand higher, touching the soft skin of her leg, the back of her calf.

"An angel of the Christian god then?" he asked, watching as small gasps escaped when his hand moved up her leg, pulling her gently closer to him. "Come to offer me salvation, sweet angel?" he asked. Salvation came in many forms, and at this moment relief from his lust would serve him well. His soul was lost, so he need not worry over that.

His angel lost her balance as he tugged on her leg, falling onto him. His breath was forced out of him, but the feel of her breasts against his chest was worth it. And now, as she lay on top of him, he was able to explore her more thoroughly.

And he did . . . wrapping his arms around her and drawing her up so that her hips and belly rubbed against the hard length of his cock. It was a glorious feeling, and his flesh swelled and readied itself for her body. His mouth watered as he grasped her shoulders and lifted her closer . . . closer to his lips.

The angel's own lips parted ever so slightly, giving him hope that the moment when he could taste her was close. Her eyes widened as she noticed his erection for the first time, and her wriggling movements—was she trying to climb off him?—simply made him harder.

Gavin fought off the sedating stupor of the healer's brew and rolled with her to his side. Smiling at her, he gazed into those dark blue eyes and saw something that looked like innocence shining back at him. The sight of it entranced him. His own soul and body were so far from that state that he hungered to touch it once more.

To touch her.

He wrapped his arm around her, cushioning her from the hard stone floor, and used his other hand to caress the soft curve of her jaw. Rubbing his thumb across her lips, he dared a first taste of her enticing mouth, holding his breath as he waited for the pleasure of it.

He swept his tongue into her mouth, seeking her own. He was overwhelmed by the kiss. Innocence was there, certainly, but also he tasted her own need and a swirl of other emotions. Gavin slanted his mouth over hers and plunged into it, tasting and suckling and searching for more of his angel. He slid his hand up into her long curls and wrapped their length around his palm, holding her close while he continued to kiss and possess her mouth.

She moved against him and he released his grasp of her hair so that he could touch her in other places. Gathering the fabric of her cloak and tunic in his hand, he pulled it up, gliding it slowly up her leg until he felt her skin there once more. The gasps she made tickled his mouth, and he continued to seek her flesh. Gavin lifted his mouth from hers only to take a breath, but got caught up in the intensity of her gaze meeting his.

Then he noticed it.

The silence.

The blessed silence in his thoughts.

The only sounds he could hear were the gasps she made each time he touched her, and the panting breaths she took in as he slid his hand between her legs and found the wetness there. If he concentrated on her, he could hear the beating of her heart and the blood rushing through her body. And he did focus on her, discovering that he could hear the tightening of her muscles and the throbbing ache pulsing in her womanly flesh.

How? How could she silence the clamor? And how could he hear such things deep within her? Things that did not have sound. Yet he could hear those and nothing else.

"Who are you?" he asked, drawing back for a moment to truly look at her face.

Even in his drug-filled stupor, he knew that she was different. But her eyes began to glaze over as his body poured out the scent that would make any woman his. Gavin felt the heat of her flesh soften beneath his fingers and moved his hand there to make her gasp as he knew she would. The sound of it echoed through the cavern and into his body.

She said nothing, his angel, only opening her legs so that he could touch her deeper. So he did, enjoying the way she arched against his hand. Gavin took her mouth, mimicking the movements with his tongue, thrusting deep and anticipating the feel of her tight channel around his prick.

The lack of clatter in his thoughts increased his desire for her and his enjoyment of the way his body felt. He knew not why or how her thoughts were hidden from him, but it was so pleasant that he laughed aloud.

"You are truly an angel," he said as he slipped his arm out from behind her and moved to kneel between her legs.

Though she did not speak, she did not object. He tugged her cloak out of his way and pulled the edge of her tunic up slowly, enjoying every exposed inch of her long legs. He leaned over and tracked kisses over her legs, still able to hear the blood as it rushed through her veins. As he approached the junction of her thighs, she touched his head.

The touch itself was a surprise because women under the control of his power usually lay compliant in his arms, allowing him his way in all things. But the clarity in her gaze when he met it was the true shock. She was not under the power of his desire.

His head swam from the effects of the healer's brew, but the rising heat in his blood battled it. Now, with her feminine scent and flesh so close, he could not stop himself. Gavin smiled at her.

"Let me pleasure you, angel," he whispered, not pausing for her permission.

Leaning down, he kissed the soft skin on the inside of her thigh as he spread her legs. Although she placed her hand on his head once more, he moved his mouth along her leg until he reached the heated place there and used his lips and tongue to tease those sensitive folds. She writhed under his attentions, and his body strained against his clothing, his skin burning to be on hers.

He'd been with hundreds of women in his life and could tell when one feigned arousal or swore to a long-lost innocence, but her body somehow tasted of it. The way she reacted, drawing away as he stroked with his tongue and then relaxing against his mouth when he pursued, spoke of a newness to this kind of passionate kiss. She did not fight him, but she did not caress him or touch him other than swirling her fingers in his hair as he moved over her.

Gavin lifted his mouth from her and massaged the now-weeping folds with his hand, sliding one finger and then two deep within her. The lack of a maidenhead spoke only of not being pure, but her body's responses revealed her lack of experience. Easing his fingers in and out, faster and harder each time, he brought her to the edge of release even while his cock and sac tightened, waiting for his pleasure. From the way her flesh pulsed around his fingers, he knew it would be well worth the time it took to ready her.

Gavin stopped, noticing again that the only sounds he could hear were those within her body. Everything else, the noise in his head, the sounds of the ocean, faded into nothing as he listened to her body sing. Her breathing quickened, her heart raced, her muscles tensed and relaxed. Every moment had its own sound to him. The only thing he could not hear was her thoughts—not as coherent words or even as the constant clatter usually in his head. He let himself go then, savoring the silence and gaining pleasure from her body, even knowing this had to be a dream.

"Ah, angel," he whispered, still surprised to hear only his own voice, "open for me." He reached down and loosened his trews. Guiding her legs around his waist, he grasped his cock and positioned himself at the opening of her tight channel. Rubbing the head of it along her cleft, he eased into her.

The feel of it—the grip as he moved deeper and deeper still—overwhelmed him, and Gavin thrust all the way in, filling her until she uttered that breathy gasp he already craved. Then she leaned her head back and released a longer moan as she reached her peak, a sound that sent icy and fiery shivers through his body and forced him closer to his release. Like an untried youth, he could feel his seed about to spill and he could not stop it. Thrusting hard and fast, he felt his entire body tighten and he waited for that moment of satisfaction, of pleasure. His angel cried out then, and he felt the spasms of the walls of her channel around his cock. He plunged once more into her and joined her in coming as his seed burst from him.

Her legs tensed around his waist and he watched the way

her lovely lips opened slightly as they both experienced the waves of release within her. The magical sounds of her release echoed in his head, sounds that reminded him of the music played on a clarsach he'd heard once as a child. It spun out around him in the air as his body found a kind of satisfaction that had always remained just out of his reach. Not only did his body soar, but his heart and soul knew a moment, a scant second, of complete peace and fulfillment.

Something he'd never felt in the arms or body of any woman before this one.

He watched a smile play on her lips as her body continued to spasm around his flesh. Slowly, she began to drift into that lethargy that follows a good bit of bedplay, but Gavin's cock remained hard and ready.

He wanted to touch that moment again . . . and again. He wanted to savor the release she gave him—release from pain, from the voices. He wanted her.

He laughed gruffly as the healer's brew began to take control of his body. He was dizzy; the strong concoction was apparently more powerful than he'd first thought. Gavin rolled off her and lay at her side, watching the rise and fall of her chest and listening to the sounds of her body, now replete with pleasure.

A breathy sigh. The calming of her racing heart. The blood slowing in her veins. The easing of the tension in her muscles and the engorgement in the flesh between her legs. All sounds he'd never been aware of and now sounds he could hear individually. And yet, the noise that usually screamed in his mind was gone.

Once his ability to hear the truth had become apparent, so had that sound—at first a constant quiet hum that he could ignore. But as his ability to hear the truth grew, so too had that noise and it worsened when he was around others, as though he was hearing all the thoughts in their minds at once, speeded up and unintelligible.

He avoided crowds, he avoided people, all in the hope of lessening the maddening pain in his head, but in vain. It seemed that as his powers grew, so did his ability to pick up the jumbled thoughts of every person in his vicinity.

Yet, now, as his limbs and eyelids grew too heavy to move, he breathed in deeply and let the silence wash over him. After months and months of pain and torment, Gavin could not fight the supreme pleasure brought by this coupling and the complete silence. Another breath and he felt sleep pulling him into its grasp.

"My angel," he whispered, both in thanks and as a plea for her to stay.

He smiled, realizing even in his stupor, she was most likely only imagined while under the influence of the healer's brew. Ah, if he had to have a dream, even one caused by herbs and ale, this was a wondrous one to have. He might have Haakon seek more of the potion after all.

Then sleep claimed him and he thought and heard nothing.

Chapter Two

Katla watched as the Truthsayer faded into sleep before she moved a muscle. Her body ached in a not-unpleasant way from his use of her, but it had been nothing like Harald's way of swiving her. That warrior had not shamed her as he could have by sharing her with his men once he had taken her maidenhead. His attentions to her were frequent, brief, and unremarkable. He'd even offered to take her as his second wife, giving her an honorable place in his household.

Nothing she'd done with Harald could have prepared her for what the Truthsayer had done. Her body had reacted under his touch like a thing unknown to her, shivering and trembling from her skin to deep inside as he caressed and kissed and even licked places she had not paid attention to before. Another ripple of pleasure shook her as she tried to move away from him without disturbing his sleep. Tugging her tunic down over her legs as she eased away, Katla sat a few feet from him and studied him now that passion no longer ruled her.

He was called Gavin of Durness, for the place where he'd been found and raised. His blond hair and light eyes spoke of Norse parentage, but none had ever claimed a link to him.

That was all she'd discovered about him, other than some rumors of his powers.

No one, none of the earl's trusted servants or men, spoke of his impairment, of the pain he suffered constantly or why he did not live on Orkney, closer to the earl's palace. Clearly, he was mad or going mad and the earl used the churning, dangerous waters of the firth that separated Orkney from the rest of the southern lands to keep him from the view of his court.

For several days, she had watched him from above, through a hole worn by the river as it flowed into his cave, observing as he dosed and drugged and drank himself into a stupor—or as he tried to. He ranted, he cursed, he called out to people not present, and he swore to any god and against all of them. When he was not yelling, he was swiving. His servant came and went each day, bringing woman after woman to serve his master's needs.

Gold seemed of no matter to him, nor did comfort or lack thereof. He lived in a cave that opened to the unruly ocean when he could live in the comforts of a noble's palace. Because of the service he provided to the earl, one of the most powerful men in the Norse world, his every whim and command was fulfilled and obeyed. If she'd not spoken to trustworthy people, people who still held her in high esteem despite her father's death and her brother's uncertain fate, Katla would never have believed some of the wild stories and rumors.

A touch of his hand during the peak of the full moon could bring forth the truth from anyone he chose. No secret could remained hidden from his ability to hear the truth within a person's mind.

She sighed, seeing no sign of otherworldly power just now. He snored loudly as though to confirm her low opinion. But, there had been a moment, when his ice-blue eyes seemed to glow with some mysterious light and when her will seemed to fade, replaced by a call that rippled through her blood. Gavin of Durness shifted then in his sleep, reaching his hand out to the place where she'd lain.

"Angel," he whispered.

So drunk that he thought her a Valkyrie first and then an angel! Katla shook her head in disbelief and looked up and down his sleeping form. Not an ounce of fat marred his body. Tight, lean muscles covered a tall frame, and she felt their strength as he'd held her and caressed her and when he pulled her on top of him. Because he'd not bothered to undress her or himself, they'd tupped in their garments so she'd seen little of his body. Now though, she realized he'd fallen asleep with his trews loosened and his cock was there for her to see. As he whispered "Angel" again, it filled and hardened as though ready once more for another bout of bedplay.

Katla smothered a laugh, afraid to bring him out of his sleep or to gain his attention again. Not afraid of swiving him, but of being discovered before she'd made all her plans. Her brother's fate now lay squarely on her shoulders, and she had little time to discover something valuable to the Truthsayer, something she could use to bargain with him for his help.

The earl used the Truthsayer's talents only for the most important matters, and her brother was not high enough in his esteem to warrant such an intervention. The Scots' king had sent questions of his own about charges of treason against her father and brother and was demanding that Kali be sent to him for judgment. Only Earl Magnus's own journey to the Norse king had delayed the matter. But on his return, expected in weeks, she did not doubt that the reprieve would end. Once Harald turned Kali over to the earl, there would be no guarantee of his safety or his life.

Standing now, she gathered her hair and tied it back. During the climb down the steep cliff to the cave, she'd lost her head cloth and the leather strap that bound her hair. No doubt the unruly mass of pale blond curls had made the Truthsayer think she looked like an angel.

She smiled then, for no one in her life had ever thought her to be such a soft creature as that. Hellion was more the claim and the curse, spoken in anger by her stepmother and her father as she tried time and time again to be more than just a daughter to the great warrior Sven of Gairsay.

And more than just the daughter of a freed slave woman who'd caught the eye of the powerful chieftain. Freeing her mother as she struggled to give birth to his child had been Sven's only act of kindness, and it was said that Katla only had status in her father's household because she resembled her dead mother so closely.

Searching around the cave, she found a blanket and covered Gavin with it.

This man was a stranger. He had used some strange power to draw her into his embrace and to make her lose her own will. At least for a short time . . . but even when her mind had cleared of the haze of his control, she could not make herself stop him.

Truly, she'd never felt anything like the sizzling sensations that pulsed through her body and soul as he touched and caressed her. Harald's attentions had not been unpleasant, but never had they caused the waves of pleasure and desire that this man had. Small spasms yet rippled deep within her, and part of her wished to wake him, to crawl back into his embrace so she could feel them again . . . and again.

Shaking her head, she forced away such thoughts and walked around him to the rocky entrance. The roar of the ocean was louder there than the rushing of the river from overhead. She shielded her eyes from the sun and searched for the small, hidden trail on one side of the entrance. Climbing down was difficult, but climbing back up along the steep and slippery path would be even more treacherous. Katla reached down, gathered the length of her tunic and gown in her hands and drew it up between her legs, making it easier to climb.

It took more than an hour to reach the top, and her chest hurt from breathing so hard. Her legs screamed from her efforts, but she pushed on, now needing to get away from the open area. She did not want his servant to see her as he sailed back to the cave. Struggling to gain her balance, Katla searched the horizon to judge how much more time before sunset. Her father's servant, now her companion, would return for her in five days' time. She had only that long to discover something she could use to gain the Truthsayer's help and prove her brother's innocence. He lacked nothing he wanted or needed. His only demands were for ale and women, and his servant fulfilled those with all haste.

What could she find that would be valuable to him?

The village of Durness lay only a few miles away, and she hoped that she could discover something about Gavin's early years there, something that would expose some need or want of his that she could fulfill in order to gain his cooperation. She had no plans past that, but the almost frantic tension inside her when she thought of Kali's fate pushed her onward.

Katla found the rocks that marked her earlier hiding place and retrieved her sack. Pulling her cloak tightly around her shoulders, she started off in the direction of the village. With the jewelry sewn into the hem of her cloak and with the coins she'd managed to hide and bring along with her, she could buy much of what she would need.

If only silver would purchase the Truthsayer's help.

If only . . .

But, five days later, she found herself with less silver than when she'd started and no more information to help her in her quest than when she'd arrived.

The day her companion would return from the north

dawned bright and sunny, and even the tumultuous sea glistened calmly beneath the sun's rays. The rare turn of weather made walking back to Gavin's cave easier than usual. She trekked along the rough path that connected Durness with the other villages scattered over the north coast, watching the sea for any sign of the small boat that would come for her.

She reached the clearing where the trail to the cave began and decided to use the time to spy on Gavin once more. Mayhap she would see something or hear something useful. Following the river as it flowed toward the sea, she soon approached the smallest of the openings in the cave's ceiling. Peering down, she searched for Gavin or his servant.

And was met by only the sound of rushing water.

When several minutes had passed with no sign or sound of people below, Katla crept to another of the ceiling holes and watched and waited once more. This one looked down nearer the sleeping area. Protected within one of the back chambers of the cave, he slept in the driest and most private part of the large dwelling. This ceiling hole looked down on the short corridor that led to it.

Nothing. No sound but that of the falling water.

Sliding back from the opening and standing, she shaded her eyes with her hand and searched the horizon to the north. A boat bobbed on the sea, still a few miles off but on its way to the shore. She had but a short time to reach the cove.

Pain sliced through her heart at that moment, for she had failed. Harald had given her a month to find the answers she sought. He'd not asked how she intended to do so, and she'd not bothered to tell him the truth of her quest. Their bargain, that she would return to live with him as his concubine in exchange for his giving her a month to pursue her search, was nearly at an end. It had taken weeks to find the Truthsayer.

The thought of her failure and what it meant to her brother and the idea of a future as nothing more than a bed warmer for one of the earl's men left a bitter taste in her mouth. Katla had seen her mother's life, empty but for the occasional attention from her father, and had vowed never to accept such a one for herself. Now, it was either save her brother or follow her mother's path to heartbreak.

Despair filled her as she watched Godrod bring the boat to shore.

"How do you fare, lady?" Godrod asked as he jumped over the side into the shallow waters and held the boat steady for her. "I have not seen such a look on your face since the day your brother was taken."

Katla pushed her hair away from her face and climbed into the boat that would take her to her unwanted fate. "I fear I have failed, Godrod, and my brother will pay with his life."

The old man smiled sadly as he helped her over the side of the small curragh. "You cannot be responsible for others, lady. Your father asked too much of you."

Tears threatened then; her throat grew tight and painful as she felt them run down her cheeks. Turning away so he and the others could not see the extent of her weakness, she watched in silence as Godrod pushed the boat free of the sand and climbed over the side to take the empty pair of oars.

Godrod and the others did not speak as they rowed away from shore and then raised the sail. It would take most of the day to sail across the straights to Orkney and then to reach Birsay on the northwestern coast of the main isle, where Harald lived on the earl's estate. Soon, though, the men began to talk among themselves, accepting that Katla wanted none of it. Only when their talk turned to the Truthsayer was she interested.

"Has he returned to Birsay, Godrod?" she asked.

"Aye, lady. The earl sent word of a dispute that needed settling and called the Truthsayer to Birsay for the full moon."

How stupid she'd been! To forget about the timing of his

power and the link to the full moon of the month. Katla had always been known as a logical and organized woman, skilled at keeping her father's household running efficiently; yet in this moment, she felt like a lackwit.

"Godrod," she said, feeling a measure of hope once more. "Do not sail to Birsay. Land on the coast a few miles away and I'll make my way there on foot."

"But, lady," Godrod began. "Harald is expecting you back."

"He gave me a month, Godrod, and it is not over yet. I cannot forsake my brother until I have exhausted all possibilities."

She watched as Godrod debated obeying her command, clearly not at peace with this change to her plans. But he'd sworn to her father to be her protector, and she depended on that oath to assure his agreement.

If Gavin the Truthsayer was going to proclaim a truth, she wanted to be there to see it. She needed to watch and discover how his power, his gift, worked. Finally, Katla released her held-in breath as Godrod nodded.

She smiled then, nodding back, and then she turned her thoughts to how she might best observe the Truthsayer without being identified. He would be taken to the earl's home and feted until the ceremony. The moon would reach its fullness in three days, so he would stay there in seclusion, she'd been told, until he was taken to the hall for the truth speaking.

If she could find a way to see him before he was taken to the ceremony. . . . If she could find a way to ask his help. . . . If she could make him believe she had something to offer in exchange for his help, then mayhap she could save Kali's life and her own future as well. For if Kali was proven innocent and inherited all that was their father's, then he would be a wealthy and powerful chieftain among the earl's men and she would once again be a prize to be bestowed upon an ally or friend.

In saving Kali she would save herself, too.

By the time they reached the shore some miles south of Birsay, Katla had the beginnings of a plan to get into the earl's home and see Gavin. This time she would speak plainly to him and surely he would see fit to help her.

Surely he would.

Chapter Three

Not even the sun glinting off the dark turquoise waters eased his spirits or the pain in his head. But it was beautiful out here on the sea, and the cool air rushing over the surface did clear his mind somewhat. He'd taken another dose of the healer's brew, but like the last four, it had not lessened his pain. Now, an hour after leaving the refuge and relative silence of the cave, he was headed for the earl's estate in Birsay. Gavin turned and looked ahead, watching as the hills of Hoy came closer and closer.

Nearly there.

He took in a deep breath and steeled himself for the coming assault. Haakon stood a short distance away on the deck of the birlinn. The earl spared no costs in gold or men to provide for his comfort and safety.

Well, he thought as he counted the number of warriors sent to accompany him, his safety was assured. His comfort was another matter.

The thoughts of just this handful of men sent dizzying waves of pain through him, but hundreds would be waiting for him at the earl's estate. Each month his dread at being near others grew stronger, as did the pain and hammering in his head. Gavin took in a deep breath and closed his eyes, trying to listen to the sounds of the sea and not the rest of it. He discovered that for a short time, he could block out the worst of it.

He could block it!

Then Gavin thought back to the first time he'd noticed he had some control over the noise and realized it had been the day after that strange yet wonderful dream. The one that included a bout of loveplay with a beautiful angel who had luminous eyes and long, curling pale hair. During that strange interlude, he could focus his thoughts and hear only the sounds of her body as they found pleasure.

And it had been a pleasure that left him satiated for the first time in as long as he could remember. His body readied itself now, just as it did whenever he brought the image of his angel to mind. It was a strange dream for many reasons, but the funniest part of it was that he'd never removed their clothes. So, though he could remember the feel of her ample breasts and the strength in her legs as she wrapped them around his waist, he could not see the color of her skin as it flushed with pleasure and he did not know if the tips of those breasts were rosy or dusky. Gavin shifted as his hardened flesh pressed against his trews once more, aching to be deep within the angel's tightness.

"Haakon," he called out without turning to face the others. When he heard Haakon's approach, he spoke without looking at him—asking the same question he'd asked for the last five days. "Was it truly only a dream?"

"I brought no one to you that day, sir. It took me several hours to return to the cave, and it was nearly full dark when I did. You were sleeping soundly from the healer's brew. And you know who has visited you since that day." No one. No one had visited since that day. He'd not asked for a woman in five days.

The words were the same as ever, repeated by Haakon every time Gavin asked him the same question. Despite his vivid memories of making love to a real woman, it had been only a dream. And though he'd consumed more of the brew, no other dreams had followed those doses, only sleep or calmness.

Gavin nodded and listened as Haakon returned to his place farther back in the boat. He'd not expected to hear a different explanation, but he could not deny that he'd hoped to. Rubbing the back of his neck, he decided that she had been an apparition. Turning away from the headwind, he called out to the man in charge of their voyage.

"How much longer to Birsay?" he asked.

The man squinted into the sun and then glanced at the land to their right side. "We cannot land at Birsay until nearly sundown, about three more hours."

The Brough of Birsay was a tidal island, separated each day from the mainland during high tide. Since the earl's estate lay close to the brough on the mainland, approaching it from the sea involved a tricky bit of timing. A smaller, shallower boat could make it, but those with a deeper hull such as this one needed a good bit of water in the adjacent bay before they could land.

It was just as well, for Gavin was in no rush to arrive. The full moon would come in half a sennight's time, and with it uncontrollable power would surge through him. His will would not be his own. When that time came, 'twas as though his own mind fled and his words were spoken by another. When he came back to himself, he carried no memory of what had been asked or answered. And no matter how much he'd searched or talked with elders from the earl's domain, or with visitors from other lands, he could never find any explanation for what occurred within him at the zenith of the full moon.

Even the Norse king's skald, well versed in stories of many cultures and lands, could provide no understanding of the power that flowed through him or the origin of it. Nor could the earl's physicians explain it or help control the pain. But worse, in the last few months, his body suffered for days and days after the truthspeaking. Not only did a deep and profound deafness occur, but his body seemed to weaken, too, more and more with each passing month.

No one knew of the deafness, and only Haakon and a few others knew the extent of the punishment his body took for being the conduit of such power. Punishment that seemed to be getting worse.

Restlessness now filled Gavin, pushing him to move along the boat as it sailed north over the calm seas. 'Twas not so large that he could walk freely, but he made his way down the center, past the mast, ducking low to avoid the sails. Reaching the back of the boat, Gavin searched the horizon behind them, gazing at the cliffs of the northern coast as they sailed farther away.

The entrance to his cave could not be seen because it lay shielded by a curve in the coastline that provided him the privacy and solitude he needed. Solitude Earl Magnus had promised he would have. The arrangement seemed to work well for them both: Magnus had someone who could settle disputes in a way that even the *Thing* could not and Gavin received the protection and patronage of one of the most powerful men in the Norse world. Unfortunately, Gavin was learning that not even a strong, influential man could keep the power he had under control. Haakon approached and waited to be acknowledged before speaking.

"You seem troubled, sir. Is there anything you need? Some

ale? Food?" The other choice was left unsaid, for it could not be accommodated on this voyage.

"Nay, Haakon. I am well."

His servant studied him, clearly with questions on his mind that he dared not ask. But, for once, the man surprised him.

"Do you think the woman was real and not conjured by the healer's potion?" The servant somehow understood how important the drug-induced dream had become to Gavin.

"I know this will not make sense," he said, lowering his voice so that the others would not hear, "but she was different from any woman I've been with before."

Gavin watched as sweat broke out on Haakon's upper lip and forehead. He looked away before speaking to Gavin, but the topic of sexual pleasure was not a comfortable one for either of them. Haakon cleared his throat and coughed before he could reply. He began and then stuttered and shook his head, not able to say the words he'd chosen. Finally, he did speak.

"Durness is not so large that she would go unnoticed, sir. I can search for her when we return there."

Stunned by the words, and the offer, Gavin shook his head. "But why would you think her real? Knowing what the healer said about the effects of his potion, why would she be other than a creature of my dream?"

He dared not hope, but still, his heart raced at the possibility his angel existed outside the realm of dreams. Now it was his turn to sweat, and he felt the beads of moisture gather on his brow.

"You slept. Soundly. For hours."

Gavin laughed. Such a mundane thing and yet it held such meaning in his life. "Aye. 'Tis true I slept." He crossed his arms over his chest. "But how does that affect her being a fantasy or being real?"

Mostly, he wanted Haakon to give him a reason to hope. To hope that his angel was real, a woman of flesh and blood. For after joining their bodies, he was able to push away the sounds that filled his mind. Something had occurred when their bodies joined that gave him a small bit of power over his growing torment. Their joining had satisfied more than just his fleshly desires; it satisfied his soul.

"You have not asked for a woman since that day."

He laughed aloud then at the irony of that statement. Most men could go days and weeks without seeking to fulfill their needs, but he barely went hours. Since the autumn of last year, his demands had increased each month. And so did his power. His ability to draw forth the truth from someone grew, as did his accuracy and his ability to hear the thoughts of others.

But now, this one woman—whether dream or real—had accomplished what none could do before, and even his servant had noticed.

"Aye, Haakon, search for her upon our return. If she is real, she may know more about the powers I hold than I have been able to discover. Seek her for me."

Haakon smiled and nodded. Nothing made the man happier than being of service. Gavin had found Haakon years before when the earl had summoned him to Orkney after hearing of his startling abilities. Haakon had served him ever since, without word of complaint or mockery for the strange style in which they lived.

Haakon bowed his head, but not before Gavin saw the satisfied expression in the servant's eyes. He watched as Haakon traced his path back to the side of the boat and stood there quietly; most likely a plan was already forming in his mind. If she existed, Haakon would track her down.

The next few hours passed and the boat skirted the edge of

Orkney, the men watching as the sun dropped lower in the sky. The Brough of Birsay with its church and outlying buildings appeared as they sailed ever nearer. Finally, under the skilled hands of the crew, their boat slid alongside the dock. Strong ropes secured the boat and all oars and sails were stowed safely. Gavin climbed over the side and waited to gain his balance before walking.

Wave upon wave of screeching, relentless clamor rolled over him. Gavin closed his eyes and tried to think about the sounds of her body once more. He recalled the silence as they coupled, her heartbeat racing, the blood pumping through her veins as her body prepared itself for him. As he thought on those sounds, the other noise receded enough for him to breathe at a normal rate and to walk without the usual dizzying pain. Haakon guided him to the path that led to the main building of the earl's estate.

Soon they arrived, and because the earl was not in residence, Gavin was able to go directly to the rooms kept for him. Luxurious for someone of common birth, his rooms included a sleeping chamber, a smaller bathing room, and even a small chamber for Haakon so that he was always nearby. The most impressive room, though, was the Hall of Disputes that Magnus had built on so that Gavin could hear arguments in privacy and with only those the earl wished present.

No matter his abilities. No matter Magnus's power in Orkney. No matter that the old gods were still respected in many places. This was a Christian land now, and powers such as his, unexplained and inconceivable to many, created fear and suspicion. Few who were not bound by oath to Magnus were permitted to observe Gavin's ritual. Most outsiders who heard of him thought him to be a master of negotiations, an accomplished bargainer who could bring opposing sides of an argument or claim to agreement and who could help the earl avoid leaving important and personal disputes to the very public and very unpredictable *Thing*.

Though stories were spun and rumors escaped, none but those who witnessed it ever knew the real method of the Truthsayer. Unfortunately for him, not even the Truthsayer himself understood exactly what happened. All he knew was the call of the full moon each month drew forth his ability to hear the truth in men's minds. Whether they wished it or not, the Truthsayer found the truth.

Gavin walked to the windows in his sleeping chamber and stared out at the bay. A few more days and he would lose more of himself. Would there come a time when there was nothing left? Each month, he noticed that his heartbeat slowed, nearly stopping when the ritual finished. Would it stop altogether one day?

Haakon entered with a cup of wine, and Gavin drank it down, holding the empty cup out for more. Though the twitching of Haakon's left eyebrow was the only indication of censure, Gavin could tell the man disapproved of his constant and increasing reliance on strong drink. It mattered not to Gavin, for whatever could ease the pain was what he would use until he could discover how to battle this affliction. Another cup appeared before him, and Gavin took it from Haakon without a word.

As he tried to concentrate on keeping the clamor at bay, he could hear Haakon in the other room, most likely unpacking his garments and readying the room for his evening meal. Gavin would eat here alone rather than join the others at their dinner. The sheer numbers of people in the hall would overwhelm him.

His rooms faced the water, with a balcony that extended over the edge of it, and were located away from the hall where everyone gathered and separate from the rest of the household.

At the worst of times, the sound of the water, crashing on the sands or against the rocky foundation of the building, eased Gavin's pain. That was why he liked the cave so much, for between the rushing of the river from the land side and the crashing of the waves from the seaside, there was so much noise surrounding him that the voices in his head faded into one blur.

"Sir?" Haakon said quietly. Gavin faced him. "Your supper will be here soon. Would you like me to invite . . ." The words faded off for there was no need to finish them.

The craving rose in his blood then. He had ignored it for as long as he could. His cock hardened in anticipation, ready to find its place deep within the heat of a woman. His skin itched and ached with the need to plow the softness between a woman's legs and make her scream out in release as he reached his. Tempted to reach down and ease the ache, Gavin nodded at his servant, knowing that the scent of his lust was already spreading through the household. In very little time . . .

The knock startled him, though it shouldn't have.

Haakon crossed the chamber and opened the door a bit, peering into the corridor and speaking quietly to someone there. Gavin's hands fisted and released as the scent of his arousal washed over him, filling the room. When the servant stepped back, he allowed a young woman to enter. Stupidly, some small part of his heart hoped to see his blond angel. Instead, a very different sort of woman stood there, her eyes glazed over from the scent his body exuded. Shorter by inches than his angel, with black hair and a thin, lithe body, this woman enticed him anyway.

Haakon looked at him, waiting for the word to dismiss her or to allow her to stay, and Gavin nodded his permission. With the ritual so near, his body wanted release, and this woman, one who'd warmed his bed before, had been very pleasing. He was certain she would be once more. He held his hand out to her and watched as she walked toward him, loosening the ties of her gown at her neck as she did.

Thora was her name and she was a slave here in Magnus's household. His mouth watered as he remembered the talents she had displayed in bedsport. Haakon disappeared without a word, trained well to do so when privacy was needed. She tugged her gown down and dropped it on the floor, barely pausing to step out of it. When she stood but an arm's length from him, she stopped and smiled. Sliding her hands up her naked body, touching and caressing her thighs and then the black curls between her legs, she reached up and cupped her breasts, lifting them as though an offering to him.

"How may I serve the earl's truthsayer?" she asked in a voice roughened by pure sexual desire. When she raised her gaze to his, it was empty. Only a blurry glow of color remained there; her will was now his to command.

Gavin hesitated for a moment, sending out his thoughts to try to hear the sounds of her awakened body, but it was for naught. The clamoring still tore through him, but he could hear nothing distinct or different from her. The touch of her hand on his chest brought him back from his thoughts.

"I would pleasure you, if you would allow it," she said, not waiting for his permission at all.

Her deft hand lifted his tunic and slipped inside his trews. Then the other one followed until soon he was fully engorged in her hands as she massaged the length of him. Gavin could not help himself in that moment. The pleasure exploded within his body and he leaned his head back and felt it course through him.

Maybe he would feel the same as he had with his dream woman. Maybe Thora could ease the ache within him and quiet the storm of noise that yet filled his mind. Maybe . . .

It was only hours later, after feverishly and desperately pursuing the same kind of satisfaction he'd found just days before and not finding it with the experienced and pleasing Thora, that he realized how empty his life had become.

And Gavin worried that his life—if he survived the coming ritual—would only get worse.

Chapter Four

Katla pulled the cloak down to cover most of her face and tried to mingle in with those entering the earl's house. The guard at the gate recognized her, allowing her to pass because he knew—as did they all—she now belonged to Harald Erlendson. Her presence was not so remarkable that he would pass the news on to Harald, so she might be able to avoid being found until she'd gotten in to see the Truthsayer.

She passed by many whom she knew, moving swiftly into the yard outside the main building and looking for a way inside. For three days she'd sought entrance without finding one. The Truthsayer was in seclusion, the gossips said. None were allowed to see or speak to him but his servant . . . and the women who saw to his needs.

Her body trembled as she thought about his needs and the way she'd responded in his embrace. Heat flushed into her cheeks, and her skin tingled as an ache pulsed deep inside her belly. Seeing to his needs would be no difficult thing at all, she thought as she fought to regain her composure. Had Sven's daughter fallen so low so quickly? Was it the whorish blood of her mother racing through her veins now, heating with just the thought of having a man's cock within her?

She wiped the sweat off her forehead with the back of her hand and searched for an unguarded door or gate. Finally, luck was with her, and she noticed one of the guards leaving his place to help a woman from the kitchens carry her burden to the midden heap. From the looks exchanged by the two as they passed her hiding place in the alcove near the door, they would not be returning soon from their task.

Katla used the guard's inattention to sneak inside the kitchen and through to the part of the house where the Truthsayer was lodged. There, she found a place to hide within one of the storage closets. When she noticed the growing darkness, she crept into the corridor and sought the hall where the guests would gather to hear his words. Using the shadows of evening to hide her movements, Katla followed close behind some others and made her way into the large chamber. Once inside, she discovered a place near the back corner where she could observe without being obvious.

This chamber was new. It had not been here the last time her father brought her to the earl's house for a feast. Plain yet elegant, the walls were not covered by the usual tapestries or decorated panels but remained unmarked. The only furniture in the room was a sturdy, throne-like chair that sat on a raised platform so that the occupant could see all those standing before him.

The man who would occupy that chair stood off to one side, alone, not conversing with the others. His gaze did not meet anyone's; he only stared at the back wall as he waited. When Brusi the Lawspeaker called out his name, he circled the chair several times before climbing the three steps to sit in it. Katla sensed a great and terrible vulnerability in him and fought the irrational urge to run to his side, to protect him somehow from what was going to happen. Just as he sat down in the chair, their gazes met for a scant second and she feared he would expose her, but a change occurred within him so quickly, she thought another had traded places with him.

His eyes began to sparkle, and even from the back of the chamber she could see their color change to something that glowed like the flashes of light during a storm. Not one color but many, rippling and pulsing as all watched. Then his face took on the look of a much younger, more unworldly man. But it was when he spoke that she was certain Gavin was no longer present and someone, or something, else sat in his place.

"Who seeks the truth?" he called out.

The voice echoed out across the chamber and it caused shivers to creep down her spine. Though she could hear something familiar in its tones, the sound of it now seemed to carry the voices of several at one time. She shook and noticed others in the room did the same.

"I do," said a man near the front. Katla stifled a gasp as her father's brother stepped closer to the Truthsayer. "I am Olaf Rognvaldson and loyal in the service of the earl."

She'd not seen her uncle since before her father's death and had not heard a word from him since. He should have been her father's staunchest supporter and yet no accusation tainted his name. Why did he stand asking for the truth to be spoken? The Truthsayer held out his hand and motioned Olaf to approach. When her uncle had climbed the first step, they clasped hands and her uncle gasped several times before standing motionless and silent.

The scene before her was nothing like what she'd expected. The two men remained without moving for several minutes until Brusi walked closer and spoke again.

"Who are you?" he asked. She noticed he did not touch either man as he asked, his attention focused now on the Truthsayer and not on her uncle at all.

"I am Olaf Rognvaldson," her uncle said once more.

"I am Olaf Rognvaldson," the Truthsayer repeated in that eerie voice that did not belong to the man she knew.

"I am Olaf Rognvaldson," they said in unison as their voices merged and melded into something frightening.

Murmurs spread through the small crowd as they realized they were witnessing an extraordinary phenomenon. Strange that not one person who'd seen the ritual had ever revealed the truth of it to her. But then, how would she ever describe the sight and sound of it to someone not present without seeming insane or possessed by some unholy demon?

"Have you sworn allegiance to Earl Magnus?" the law-speaker asked.

"I am sworn to Magnus Einarson," the men answered in their melded voice.

"Do you keep your word of honor, Olaf Rognvaldson?"

"Aye. My word is my bond," the voice answered.

Katla shook then, unable to watch without reacting to the power that seethed and surged before her. Brusi looked at Harald before continuing his questions, and Harald whispered something to him. The old man called out again.

"Did you play a part in your brother's treason?" he asked.

Katla wanted to scream out and declare her father's innocence, but she was now among enemies. And she needed to fulfill her father's last command to save her brother. She bit her tongue to keep the words in her mouth and waited to learn more.

"Nay," they answered as one. "I knew not of his plans."

Covering her mouth with her hand, Katla trembled and shook. His words would seem to confirm the worst about her father, but yet there was some room for another truth. And he'd said nothing of her brother or his role. Surely, Kali was too young to have been drawn in to any dangerous plot?

She watched as Harald whispered some other words to Brusi, who repeated the question to the Truthsayer.

"Can you be trusted to control the lands and goods and slaves of Sven Rognvaldson in the name of the earl?"

She shook her head at the question. Her uncle would gain everything her father had fought and worked for in his life. How could Olaf be so disloyal to his own brother? Thinking back, Katla knew the answer—for his own gain and to increase his own wealth and status. The man would swear and promise to anyone if he stood to gain from such a declaration. And, oh, he would gain so much in this matter.

"I can."

Two words shattered her hopes. Two words took everything in her world and placed it in the hands of this *nithing*, who would step over nephews and nieces to take all. Two words robbed her of any hope she could prove her brother's innocence, for her uncle had made it clear he would be his brother's heir.

"Is that the truth?" the lawspeaker asked. Katla held her breath, praying for something that she knew would not happen.

"The truth has been spoken," they said together. Then, the Truthsayer released her uncle and said once more in that unnatural voice, "The truth has been spoken."

The tension that held those in the room captive began to ease as the Truthsayer began to change back into the man Gavin. Her uncle stepped down but remained at the front of the room as though waiting for something else. The lawspeaker called out in a loud voice to those watching.

"Earl Magnus is satisfied with the oath of Olaf Rognvaldson and bestows on him all of the lands and goods and slaves forfeited by Sven the Traitorous at his rightful death."

"Nay!"

The word was out of her mouth before she could think, and it drew the attention of everyone in the room to her. She stood tall then and called it out once more. Someone must challenge this terrible injustice. "Nay!"

The crowd parted before her, and she watched Harald's shocked reaction as she strode quickly to the front. The perfect person to prove her brother's innocence still sat motionless on his chair, and she would demand that he help her now. She had nothing to bargain with, but surely a demand for true justice before so many men of honor would not go ignored.

"Call my brother, Harald. Let the Truthsayer speak his truth."

The only one who could help was changing before her eyes from Truthsayer to man, and her heart sank as she realized she'd missed her chance. "I beg you to hurry! There is not much time."

Chaos erupted in the room as those watching the ritual recognized her and her uncle demanded she be taken away. Harald grabbed her by the arm and tried to pull her out of the chamber, but she dug her heels in and struggled against his superior strength. A single voice stopped everything. Still part otherworldly but growing more human, it caused everyone to turn toward the Truthsayer. The wild glow faded from his eyes, and the countenance became familiar once more.

"She is mine," Gavin called out.

"Truthsayer," her uncle interrupted. "Katla is the daughter and the sister of traitors and should be put to death like them."

"She is mine," he repeated louder. "Harald," he began, but his words faltered as he seemed to lose his balance. "Bring her to me in three days."

Stunned by his words and even more when Harald nodded, Katla gave in. Harald dragged her from the chamber, calling out orders to the earl's men to clear the chamber. When he thrust her into the arms of two strong warriors, she had no choice but to go. She tried to see what had happened to the Truthsayer, but the men dragged her down the corridor and out of the building before she could.

Now, she needed someone to save not only her brother but herself, and she knew there was no one who would intervene on her behalf.

She was real!

A frigid chill began to seep into Gavin's flesh, and he fell back into the chair from which he'd tried to rise. Haakon cleared the chamber quickly, and Gavin could do little more than watch as the witnesses were herded into the next room to be instructed on what they were and were not permitted to say about the ritual. In just minutes, he sat in the empty and silent chamber, waiting for the worst of the aftereffects to happen. His stomach clenched as the first wave of utter, devastating pain shot through his ears and encircled his head.

Not even his attempts to focus on the woman, the real woman, helped him then. A burning unlike the heat of any flame began deep within his ears, filling his head. Gavin covered his ears with his hands and tried not to moan against the pain. Others were still in the corridor, and he wished no one to hear or see the full extent of the effects. But soon, his efforts failed and he fell to the floor, writhing in torment as the heat burned and burned.

His lungs refused to draw breath and he felt the beat of his heart slow. Just as he thought it would stop altogether, it beat once more . . . and then again . . . and again, until he knew it would not cease.

The pain of the thoughts that invaded his mind was nothing compared to this weakness. He fell in and out of consciousness from the intensity, unable to bear it or fight it. Minutes or hours passed, he knew not which, for pain was the only constant. Over and over it returned to its highest level and then ebbed to something less.

At some point, as he regained consciousness, he thought the worst might be past. He had not the strength to move or even to lift his head, so he lay as he'd fallen and waited, knowing that Haakon would come in to help him. But he knew that once the burning ceased, the chaos of hearing the thoughts of others would strike him. The clear individual thoughts of anyone within miles would begin whispering in his mind and then rise to a steady stream of voices, all demanding he listen, all competing within his head and driving him slowly mad.

It would begin soon. If he had regained enough of his wits that he could focus his thoughts, it was nearly time. The strangest part of the aftereffects had happened already.

He was deaf.

His ears were burned out of their ability to hear.

It would be days before his hearing returned. All he could do was wait and pray he was right about the timing of things. The pattern had established itself months ago, growing now as each month passed and rushing toward some pinnacle of pain and power near the end of October, if his calculations were correct. And then, he knew not if he would survive at all, with or without the power that now punished him with every use of it.

But for now, all he had the strength to do was lie still and wait for the inevitable.

They had not used undue force, but Katla felt battered and bruised by the time the guards tossed her into a small, windowless room at the end of one hallway near Harald's quarters in the earl's house. His own home was a short distance inland from here, but he stayed in the earl's household when on duty and especially when the earl was away from Birsay. She felt her way around in the dark and then sat against the wall in the corner away from the door.

The barred-from-the-outside door.

Exhaustion set in as she waited there for Harald to come to her. She knew he would once he'd seen to his duties. And she did not look forward to their encounter. Though he was slow to anger and had not brutalized her in any way, she feared his reaction to her interference. Katla leaned her head against the wall at her back and tried to rest.

Would Harald relinquish her to the Truthsayer? Would he use her first? Was he angry that she'd interfered? Too many doubts and questions plagued her for her to get any rest, so she simply waited to meet her fate. Rubbing her arms, she knew that bruises would be showing before long. If those were the only injuries she sustained this day, she would count herself lucky.

Hours passed and her stomach rumbled, reminding her of missed meals and other needs. She'd never been one to skip any meals happily, enjoying both the food and the company. Now, she had neither.

At times like this, she mourned deeply all that she'd lost. But just as tears threatened, the noises in her stomach interrupted, reminding her that she had no time or strength for grief or feeling sorry for herself.

The household quieted around her and still she waited.

Just as she began drifting off to sleep, she heard footsteps approaching down the corridor. Heavy, male footsteps that paused at the door of her prison. She pushed herself to her feet, wanting to meet whoever came at her standing. Katla shoved her hair away from her face and over her shoulders and straightened up to her full height.

Would it be Harald who opened the door? Mayhap her uncle, seeking to clean up one more loose end left by her father? If Katla was not alive to try to prove Kali's innocence, there would be no one left to challenge Olaf's right to his brother's holding.

Clenching her fists at her sides, she took several deep breaths. She listened as the bar was lifted and tossed aside, the sound echoing through the tiny room. Then the door opened and a man's form filled the doorway.

"How does the Truthsayer know you, Katla?"

Chapter Five

He led her out of the small room and down the corridor to his chambers without saying another word, but anger rolled off him in palpable waves as they walked. A few turns and he opened another door, then waited for her to enter ahead of him. When he'd closed the door, Harald crossed his arms over his chest and stared at her. Katla searched for the right words to say, but Harald did not wait.

"How does the Truthsayer know you?"

Katla hesitated, certain that Harald would never approve of her attempts to get the Truthsayer's help. Or her sharing her body with him.

"I sought his aid, Harald. You gave me a month to find a way to help Kali."

"He uses women for one purpose only. Did he use you, Katla?" Strange how men never considered their own actions when judging another's.

"And you, Harald? Did you not use me in the same way?"

"Before I even touched you, I offered you a place in my household. I do not use women and toss them aside. Is that treatment fit for the daughter of Sven Rognvaldson?"

"Sven the Traitor?" she asked, the words bitter in her

mouth. "How will I live if my brother is executed and my uncle claims all that should be Kali's?" She turned and walked away from him, trying to control the anger now building within her.

"As your concubine? Warming your bed when you have a need for me? How is that different from the Truthsayer's plans for me?" She faced him then. "Worry not, Harald. He will not keep me for long. He never keeps any woman for more than a day or two. Once he tires of me, I will be yours once more."

She'd not realized how angry she was at the idea of being passed from man to man as though only a thing to be used. Her heart raced as she gave vent to the feelings for the first time since watching her father die.

"Did you order your man to kill my father so you could have me, Harald? Was it part of the earl's plan? Your plan mayhap?"

He raised his hand and Katla expected to feel the blow. She didn't realize she'd close her eyes until she peeked from beneath her lids to see if he'd come closer. Harald stood only an arm's length from her, his arm raised to strike. His face was flushed with anger, but his eyes revealed an emotion he'd never shown her before. He dropped his arm and let out a long, exasperated breath.

"I have wanted you for years, Katla. I admit it freely. But I did not kill your father to get you. I bargained with him as any man does."

The words did not make sense for several seconds, but when their meaning became clear, Katla gasped. "He would never have done so!" she cried out. "I was to be wed to Einar's son Bjarni next spring."

"You were to be given to me after the harvest. If I agreed to help him kill Earl Magnus so your father could take his place."

Katla staggered back and landed hard against the wall. It could not be true! She shook her head violently, as though the action would negate the accusations made. Sven had always been loyal to the earl, fighting his battles, enjoying his rewards, and living a full life on Gairsay. Why would he have even considered such a path?

But in that same moment, she knew the answer to her own question. More wealth. More power. More lands. More.

Her stomach rolled as she thought of all the implications of this new knowledge for her and her brother.

Her father was a traitor.

Before she understood what was happening, Harald wrapped his arm around her waist and dragged her to the pot kept beneath the stool in the corner. Her stomach emptied on its own as shock, disappointment, and fear coursed through her. Finally, when she was able to sit back on her own, Harald walked to the other side of the room, poured a cup of water, and brought it to her. She wiped her mouth with the back of her hand, hoping her stomach's rebellion was done. As she rinsed her mouth, Harald strode across the room and then just watched her.

"He spoke to you directly about his . . . plan?" she asked. Katla needed to know more about this plot, because deep within, she did not believe Kali was part of it.

Harald nodded. His blue eyes stared intently at her, as though searching for something. "Aye. Several times. Each time his words seemed more enticing and more interesting. You were the final bargaining piece offered to me."

She swallowed several times but could not get out the myriad of questions that his comment caused.

"He'd noticed my interest in you, Katla. Sven knew that several of Magnus's men hungered for you. He decided I was the most worthwhile to approach with his offer."

And she'd never noticed his interest. Katla had known Harald only as the earl's man. She'd never thought his attempts at conversation or the greetings he spoke to her were anything more than the respect of a man for the kin of an ally. Worse, she'd thought her father would approach Bjarni's father as he'd promised. She'd thought . . .

Many things that were false.

"You refused him?" Katla pushed her hair from her face, twisting the length of it in her hands and then tying it into a knot behind her head. "But now you have me anyway."

"I wanted you in an honorable bargain for an honorable place in my household. You would be respected as my second wife, not a prize for breaking my bond to the earl. And not to be used and tossed aside like the scraps from a half-eaten meal." *As the Truthsayer will do* was left unsaid.

From the first, she'd sensed Harald's honor. She'd used it to save Kali that morning, and now she understood more about the man before her. She might be mistaken or naïve, but Katla thought she heard some bit of softness in his words and in his tone. Harald wanted her only for personal reasons, not to advance himself or to profit from her. His gruff manner and awkward behavior hid feelings he could not readily speak of.

But his feelings and desires aside, there was one question she feared and needed to ask.

"Was Kali involved, Harald? Tell me the truth, I beg you."

Katla prepared herself for the worst, fearing that she would hear more terrible truths about the family she thought she knew. Her hands trembled, so she entwined her fingers and held them tight. Taking a deep breath, she met his gaze and waited.

Harald returned to where she sat on the floor and crouched before her, bringing himself down to her level. His gaze softened, and the urge to cry overwhelmed her. She shook her head, not wanting to hear the truth he would speak. It would be better not to hear her brother called traitor by the man with whom she would spend her life. Now that she knew the truth about her father and his life, she realized his end was a kinder one than he probably deserved. But her brother? Not Kali.

Harald reached out and touched her cheek with a gentle caress. Then he lifted her face up so that he looked upon her. He rubbed the tear that spilled from the corner of her eye with his thumb, and then a sad smile touched his mouth.

"I do not know, Katla," he whispered to her. "Your father did not speak of Kali during our talks." Katla blinked away the tears. Kali was innocent! But Harald's next words dashed her feeble hopes. "But others have laid accusations against him."

Katla realized why Harald had spared her brother that morning—he had no problem with the killing of her father because he knew Sven was guilty of treason, but he had no such proof against her brother. "That is why you spared him?" she asked.

"Aye. Because I knew not whether the accusations were real or stemmed from the jealousy of others."

"My uncle?"

"Aye. He stood to gain much if both Sven and his son were gone. I doubted his honor and decided to wait before executing Kali. To give Olaf a chance to prove himself."

"And to give me a chance to prove Kali innocent?"

He dropped his hand and stood in front of her, helping her to her feet.

"I am only a man, Katla. A man who wanted a woman and was given the chance to have her. Do not make this out to be more than that."

His voice roughened, making her suspect he tried to make less of the reasons behind his actions. Harald wanted her. But would he still want her knowing she'd already given herself to the Truthsayer and would again if he turned her over in three days as ordered?

"And now, Harald Erlendson? Do you still want me, knowing I have shamed you by lying with another man?"

His eyes hardened with what Katla thought was jealousy.

"He has some power over women that steals their will and makes them bend to his desires. I have seen it happen before. I do not hold you responsible for falling under his spell. Nor will others."

Was that what had happened? Katla recalled her feelings when she'd found the Truthsayer nearly unconscious in his cave. She had felt strangely compelled by his touch and his voice, but never believed she could not have walked away or refused his attentions. Calling it some otherworldly compulsion took the responsibility off her shoulders. Looking at Harald now, she understood it would be easier between them if he accepted whatever happened between his concubine and another man as something that could not have been avoided.

Partly out of respect for this man who'd wanted her in spite of her father's actions and partly because she simply did not have the strength to argue, she nodded and accepted his excuse for her behavior.

"Will you give me to him as he's demanded then?"

Harald nodded and turned away from her, but not before she saw the way his hands gripped into fists and his jaw clenched. She knew his answer before he spoke the words.

"Aye, Katla. My wishes do not matter when the earl's truthsayer wants what or who I have. I must do as he's asked in order to fulfill my duty to the earl."

He surprised her by striding over to her, pulling her into his arms, and kissing her with more desire than he'd ever done before. Like a man hungering for that which he needs, he plundered her mouth, his tongue stroking deep inside her mouth to find and touch and taste her own. He tangled his hand in her hair and held her face to his so that she could not move away and break the kiss.

Harald turned his face, angling his lips against hers. He took several steps, backing her up against the wall, and never lifting his mouth from hers. Caught between the wall and his body, Katla felt his hardness against her belly.

Would he take her? Now, before the Truthsayer laid claim to her body?

When he finally lifted his mouth from hers, he kissed and nipped at the skin of her neck as she dragged in a breath. Harald rubbed himself against her and the passion in this embrace, in this kiss, surprised her. His attentions to her had always been calm and almost impersonal. This, this spoke of a crushing need and overwhelming desire.

He released her hair and slid his hands to the neckline of her gown, pulling it free and tugging it until her breasts were bared to his gaze. He was out of breath, too, but he only paused for a moment before drawing one of them into his mouth, playing with its tip until it tightened. Then he moved to the other and suckled it until it hardened. Unable to breathe at such pleasure, she watched as he placed his mouth on the sensitive skin near the nipple and suckled on it. The bite of his teeth there caused her to gasp, but he soothed the small dash of pain with his tongue and lips. Her head fell back against the wall and she moaned, for it was a pleasurable sensation and it caused wetness to gather between her legs.

He'd never done such a thing before and that place deep inside ached from it. Her hips rocked against his cock on their own, and waves of pleasure pulsed there—just from Harald's mouth on her breast.

Then, as quickly as it had started, it ended. Harald released her and stepped back, drawing his fingers through his beard and rubbing his face with his hands. He turned from her and her body screamed out a protest, throbbing and wanting release.

"Harald?" she asked, breathless with need and desire. "Will you not have me?"

He reached down and adjusted his trews before shaking his

head in reply. "Nay. He swived you and will again and I would know if you carry his child before taking you back into my bed."

Shame doused her desire quickly. Though she understood his actions, they hurt anyway. She began to gather the edge of her gown together when he nodded at her.

"And I have marked you there so that he knows you belong to someone else."

Katla glanced down and saw the mark, the darkening bruise on her breast where Harald had sucked and bitten with his teeth. Indeed, with her pale skin, the mark would be visible for days to anyone who saw that place on her body.

As the Truthsayer would, if Harald was correct about his intentions.

She reached up and touched the skin there, causing her nipple to pucker against the cloth of her gown. She shivered then, her body readied for a passion that was not to be.

Harald walked to the door and opened it. He spoke in a low voice to someone in the corridor before turning back to her.

"You will stay here until I come for you. Do not leave," he said in a harsh voice. "Where is Godrod?"

"In the village." She went to Harald and laid her hand on his arm. "I still need to prove my brother's innocence. Mayhap the Truthsayer will . . ."

"Use his power for your brother's sake? Nay, Katla, do not even wish for it."

"I will ask him to do so. Surely . . ."

Harald shook his head and snorted. "Women serve one purpose to him, Katla. Do not mistake your place or importance. Besides, the earl would not permit it."

"If the earl seeks justice, he will," she stated in a tone far bolder than she felt as she watched Harald's expression.

"The Truthsayer is given the power but once a month during the full moon. He only hears the truth of one person, one person chosen by the earl. Magnus has a surfeit of crucial matters to use that power on."

"But my brother?" Katla argued. "His life is important."

Harald closed the door and shook his head.

"The earl believes your brother to be a traitor just like his father was. He will not *waste* the power of the Truthsayer to prove what he believes he already knows."

"But . . ." she interrupted. He waved off her protest.

"With tonight's declaration, everything that was your father's is now Olaf's, so Magnus has no pressing reason to search for proof. Olaf is an experienced warrior with men who will follow him into battle and do his bidding. Your brother is an unknown youth, unproven in battle or in manhood or in honor. Why would he be of significance to the earl?"

Katla could not argue with Harald's logic or his knowledge of the situation or the earl. Her brother was important only to her. "Then why did you let me seek proof of his innocence?"

A hint of a smile lightened his intense face.

"Because I know you believe in it and I wanted you to be at peace in your life with me."

He was a good man beneath the bluster.

A good man. An honorable man. A man who would take her once the Truthsayer wanted her no longer. She could do worse.

The moment spun out between them until someone knocked on the door and Harald opened it. A slave entered, carrying a tray of food.

"Do not try to leave, Katla," he said as the slave put the tray down on the table in the corner. "I will speak to you on the morrow."

Harald followed the slave out and closed the door behind him. Katla walked to the door and opened it a crack. A guard stood there, ensuring that she would not leave. A glance at the window showed it to be too small for her to climb through, if she was intent on escape.

The aroma of a hearty stew caught her attention, and her stomach growled in hunger. She laughed and decided that no matter what she faced, she would rather face it with a full stomach. After she'd eaten the stew and crusty bread without even pausing to drink any of the ale in the cup, her exhaustion roared up and she sought sleep on top of the bed.

Though she thought Harald might return to sleep with her there, when Katla next awoke, the rising sun lit the room. The other side of the bed was cold and unused.

Harald had slept elsewhere.

Chapter Six

The voices began as the night gave way to dawn. At first, he mistook them for real voices, and he awoke to answer their questions. But then, as the potions wore off, Gavin realized they were only phantoms. He recognized some of the voices, for they belonged to people he knew in the village. Others he did not know, though each one was as clear as if the speaker stood before him, awaiting his reply.

The first days after the ritual were horribly confusing for him. With his own hearing gone and the voices so clear in his mind, it was difficult to know when he was really speaking to others and when he was talking to the air around him. Haakon did his best to guide him by gestures and expressions, but too many times he found himself receiving questioning looks from those nearby.

On those days, before all the voices blended back together, he often appeared mad. Driven out of his mind by the pain and power.

Gavin forced himself from bed and stood on the balcony now, watching the sea as the tide receded. A fisherman's wife berated her husband about yesterday's catch. The miller considered charging more to mill the grain of the baker. The guard at the gate was exhausted from too much drink and too much swiving. A child cried out for her mother. He heard them all.

He thought that, sometimes, it was worse when he struggled against the voices, when he tried to block them out. Now, if he acknowledged them, even in his thoughts, they seemed to fade to something less threatening. But as the village and the earl's household woke for the new day, hundreds and hundreds of voices joined the chorus in his mind and the true pain began, reminding him of how little power he really held. When one voice stood out from the rest, asking about his food, he shook his head and replied aloud.

"Nay," he said, turning to face the slave who'd asked, "I want no more porridge."

Instead of a kitchen slave checking on his morning meal, he found a young woman cleaning his bedchamber, who stared at him with a frightened expression in her wide blue eyes. When their gazes met, she quickly lowered hers. Since he could not hear his own voice, he suspected that he had yelled his inappropriate answer too loudly, scaring her into believing the stories told about him.

He went mad during the days after the full moon.

He screamed and ranted at people not present and at words not spoken.

He ensorcelled women if they looked deeply into his eyes and then took their wills and bodies for his own evil purposes.

Clearly, she believed the last one and it was partly the truth. But not this morn and not her. He had found the angel of his dreams and she would be his soon.

"Go," he said, watching as she quickly dropped the rags and bucket to the floor and scurried from the room.

Too loud? Too angry? He could not control his voice because he could not hear it. Frustrated, he cursed, bringing Haakon running.

"Take this away now," he said to Haakon, pointing at the remnants of his morning meal.

Haakon forgot about the deafness and began speaking. Gavin shook his head and waved him out. Completely exhausted from the ritual and the flow of power in his body, he needed rest more than anything. If not for that need, he would be buried up to his balls in the tightness of the woman he'd heard called Katla.

He barely made it to the side of the bed before falling onto it. If his cock could stand, he would have her now, but he surrendered to his weakness and fell deeply asleep for hours, waking only for another meal and then more sleep. His sleep was disturbed by the din of the voices, so the only time he could get much rest was at night, when others were sleeping, too. Fortunately, he could not hear dreams.

Gavin lived a foggy and blurry existence until the third day after the ritual. He'd demanded she be brought to him then only because his hearing usually began to return by the third day, but when he awoke that morning and could hear only the thoughts of others, he knew he'd made a mistake.

Unaccustomed to becoming deaf for days at a time, he had not the skill of reading facial expressions or lips. So he avoided others until it passed. His excitement at finding her had caused him to make an error in judgment, yet he could not forget the thrill he'd felt when he'd caught sight of her.

Though he wanted to ask Haakon for details—he had no doubt that his servant had learned all about her—there was not point until he could hear. Now, it was time to summon her and he only hoped he did not embarrass himself too badly in front of her.

Haakon had a bath brought, and the steaming water soothed Gavin. He was so weak that he had to rest afterward, but he felt the excitement within him growing as the time for Katla's arrival approached. He'd sent a message to Harald to present her after the evening meal, but his stomach was in knots and he could not eat a bite. Even the constant chatter in his head did not lessen his anticipation of seeing her again . . . of having her again . . .

But most of all, of hearing only the sounds within her as they coupled.

He laughed then, drawing the attention of the slaves in his chamber who were readying it for the night. Had he imagined that part of their encounter? Had it been the potion? Gavin dared to hope now that he knew she was real. Mayhap she could help him tame the pain and the voices? This time, his laughter was louder and even Haakon turned to him.

Evening came, the sun set, and the lamps were lit. He paced the length and breadth of the chamber, waiting for her. His body was recovering and his cock hardened more with each passing minute. He did not hear the knock, but caught sight of Haakon opening the door. Taking a deep breath, he watched as she entered.

As before, she stood there like a Valkyrie, tall and proud, with her hair in a long braid. Walking toward him, she would not meet his gaze, staring instead at the floor as Harald escorted her in. Although Gavin had no skills in reading faces, Harald's glare told him much. Possession sat deep in his expression. And jealousy and anger. Though they never touched each other as they walked or stood waiting, even Gavin could feel the ties between them.

Gavin looked from one to the other, and then Haakon said something to both of them. Harald glared at him but nodded and turned to leave. Then he paused and took Katla's hand and spoke to her. Damn! Gavin could not hear the words, but she trembled when he finished and nodded. Now, she would not look up at him.

"Katla," he said.

She startled and said something, but Haakon interrupted before he could make another mistake. When she did glance up at him, he read the fear in her eyes and hated it.

"Do you fear him or me?" he asked.

She looked toward the door through which Harald had just left and shook her head in reply.

"Do you fear me then?" he asked, hoping he was not the cause for the distraught expression on her face now.

She glanced up for a moment and then down at her hands, which were clasped before her. Then she shook her head again.

"Haakon, leave us," he ordered. The servant did as he was told, and within a minute they were alone.

"Do you fear what will happen between us? Did you dislike being with me?"

He was not sure why he asked the question when he could not hear the answer, but he waited for something, a sign from her that it was not him or what they had shared that frightened her. He had heard the sounds of her body as it peaked with his and thought she had enjoyed it, but he could not be sure.

It seemed like an eternity passed before she responded in any way. Then he saw a blush creep up her face and, with the tip of her tongue, she licked her lips. His erect cock throbbed in his trews as he stood and walked the few paces to where she waited.

Her eyes met his and she smiled then, just a slight uplifting at the corners of her mouth, but it was enough for him. Gavin felt his whole body ready itself as he held his hand out to her. The musky scent of his arousal began to spread and he noticed that her eyes glazed over for a moment, then brightened once more.

She would not be bent to his will like the others. He wanted it to be her choice. Anticipation sang through his veins and his heart raced in excitement.

The voices in his head also surged then, too many at once for him to listen to, distracting him from her. Gavin forgot for a moment that only he heard them.

"Leave me alone!" he shouted. "Give me some peace!"

To his horror, Katla flinched and backed away from him. She was turning when he realized what he'd said. He reached for her, grasping her arm and tugging her back to face him. In what he hoped would be a whisper, he pleaded with her.

"Katla, I did not mean you. Stay with me this night."

Then, two voices pushed forward, screaming out the same words at him: *Do not hurt her!* The voices were so clear, he was sure the speakers stood right behind him.

Gavin clenched his head in his hands and turned to face those who would think him capable of doing so. "I will not hurt her! Now leave me be!"

No one stood nearby.

Gavin closed his eyes, mortified at the insane display she'd witnessed. How could he explain it to her? Should he even try?

The touch of her hand on his back surprised him. He turned and found her close by. Her mouth moved but he heard nothing. Hel! But when she stroked his arm in a gesture that could only be described as comforting, his heart dared to hope that she could be trusted with the worst about him.

"Are you unwell?" Katla asked.

She noticed that he watched her mouth as she spoke but did not answer her. Mayhap he was still caught up in whatever had controlled him during the ceremony three days ago?

She did what she felt she should, what she'd wanted to do when he looked so vulnerable as the power entered him that night. Katla continued to stroke his arm, trying to soothe the wildness she saw in his gaze. When he stared into her eyes, she noticed the scent in the air around them, as she had in the cave.

"Stay with me," he said in a low voice. "Lie with me."

Ripples of desire, unknown to her until the first time he'd touched her, made her skin tingle and the tips of her breasts tighten.

"Stay with me," he repeated, stepping closer and leaning down until their mouths nearly touched. The next words tickled her lips as he spoke, but with lust, not amusement.

"Lie with me, Katla." He tilted his head then and whispered once more against her mouth. "My angel."

The pause between asking and taking was gone before she could even reply, but her body had answered for her. At his plea, her body ached and throbbed deep inside, the blood pooling in her womb as her hips arched against his body. Her head spun as she breathed in the scent swirling around them and as his mouth finally, finally, claimed hers.

Katla found herself gripping his arm as he took her mouth by storm. His tongue invaded and tasted and caressed. He suckled her tongue, drawing it into his own mouth, then guiding her to do the same with his. He laughed, a deep and wholly male sound of lust. When she grabbed hold of his other arm, pulling him against her, she felt his chuckle against her mouth and through her body.

"Katla," he whispered when he lifted his lips from hers. He licked and kissed his way down her neck, whispering her name over and over between each touch of his tongue or lips.

"Katla." A kiss.

"Katla." A caress by his hot tongue.

"Katla." He suckled the skin at the base of her neck.

She thought he might be repeating it to remember her name among those of the countless other women he'd coupled with. Regardless of the reason, the sound of her name on his lips sent shivers of pleasure over her skin and waves of longing into her heart. Harald's warning not to expect more than a tupping from the Truthsayer echoed in her thoughts as Gavin reached up and undid the leather ties holding her hair.

She dropped her hands to her sides, enjoying the way he ran his hands through her hair and massaged her head. Closing her eyes and allowing him his way, she reveled in the decadent and pleasing sensations. He must have known, for he chuckled again, the sound rumbling deep in his chest. Katla smiled, for even though the bedplay between her and Harald had never been filled with laughter or touching, this pleased her.

"I would see you garbed in nothing but your hair, angel."

The request and the way in which he said it made her body throb anew. Nakedness was not so strange a thing for her, but to play this way instead of simply joining was. She opened her eyes and saw the intensity of his gaze and knew she wanted to please him. Before she agreed, he spoke again.

"I want you, Katla. I want you to return to the Southerlands with me until the next full moon."

Shocked that he wanted her in his bed for more than just this night, she began to back away. But he took her in his arms and held her close.

"I will grant your every desire and pleasure you in ways you have not imagined if you will come with me." He kissed her again, stealing her breath and her will to refuse. Her body ignited with lust at his words and his kiss. "Anything you ask shall be yours if I can grant it."

In that moment, the Truthsayer had revealed the one thing he wanted that only she could provide. She did not understand what drove his desire for her or his reasons for thinking she was any different from every other woman he'd taken to his bed . . . but he did.

"Would you use your powers to hear my brother's truth?"

The words flowed out before she thought on them. But, if he agreed, then she would gladly whore herself to fulfill his desires.

He never paused in replying either. "Whatever you ask, Katla." He kissed her again and the scent increased around them. "Whatever will please you."

Chapter Seven

Whatever the cost, he would pay it.
Whatever her price, he would meet it.
Gold mattered little to him. Power even less. But the value of the silence she brought to his mind was beyond measure and worth anything she would demand in return. And the fact that he could not hear what she asked of him bothered him not a bit.

As soon as her body began to respond to his touch, he could push the voices from his mind. That respite was worth any price she might ask.

When she raised her hands and unpinned the brooches from the apron-like tunic of her gown and then pulled the garment over her head, he had his answer and more. From the way in which she moved, hesitant and unsure, he suspected she'd not done something like this before. He wanted to reach over and rip everything else off, but he kept his desire under control and stepped back so that he could watch her as she moved.

Katla loosened the undergown and unlaced the ties down the front of it. He waited, aching to touch her flesh, to taste her essence and to feel the grip of her inner muscles as she rode him to pleasure. When she paused as though unsure, he directed her.

"Open your gown, Katla. Let me see your breasts."

She tugged on the opening in her gown and spread it wide until he could see both of her full breasts. The nipples were tight buds of a pale, rosy shade, and his mouth watered to taste them. The sight of the bruise stopped him.

"Who did that?" he asked. His voice must have been louder than he thought, for she flinched. She lifted her hand to cover the lovemark near her nipple, and the movement sent a new fire through his body.

He read the name she spoke on her lips. Harald.

Jealousy pierced him when he realized that Harald had been the man before him, the one who had taken the prize of her virginity and the one to whom she would return when they were finished. But she was his now and when she left, she would remember the things they did together; she would remember his touch and his kiss, and he would leave his mark on her for Harald to find and wonder about.

Dangerous male jealousy fed his desire for her, and he decided to make this passion last between them. To stretch out their pleasure until they were weak with desire and then to quench it, over and over this night and for as many as she or the fates would grant him.

Did she think of Harald's touch when it was his hands caressing her? Well, he would pleasure her until she could think of only himself when she thought of coupling with a man. Until she wore his scent, his taste, his mark, and his seed on her and in her.

"Hold your breasts out to me," he ordered. She obeyed him, sliding her hands under her breasts and lifting them out of the gown to him. "Rub your thumbs over the tips."

Gavin could hear her every gasp in his mind, the blood

rushing to her loins, the skin of her breasts tingling as she touched the sensitive buds and made them sing. He gasped as the pleasure of it poured over him. "Again."

Her body bucked this time, feeling the same pleasure that he could hear and see. She did it again without his asking and then again. Gavin saw and heard the moan that escaped her mouth that last time, and before he could stop himself, he dropped to his knees in front of her and took one nipple into his mouth, suckling and biting it until she moaned over and over again. Relentless now, he moved to the other, wrapping his arms around her to keep her standing as he teased and tormented until he could hear her blood racing beneath her skin. Gavin leaned back then, unwilling to push her body too fast to completion.

"Hold them again," he ordered, for her hands had slipped to his shoulders.

Katla lifted her breasts to him again, able to refuse but also not willing to miss the pleasure he'd promised her. The scent of him invaded her limbs and her mind, and she sank into its control and his. Her breasts ached for more and the tips still throbbed from his mouth. He lifted his hands and rubbed his thumbs across them. Her legs wanted to give out, but she fought to stand. Leaning against his hands, her entire body pulsed as he rubbed harder and faster against them. Then he took each tip between his finger and thumb and rolled them, flicked them, and then tugged until she screamed.

Like invisible strings, each touch pulled and vibrated against something deep within, causing her heart to race and her blood to heat and pulse. Her womb felt heavy with pleasure, and a tension built within her until she thought she would come undone. Then the worst thing happened—he stopped again and moved away from her. She reached out to keep him close, but he shrugged off her hold and stood.

"Please?" Her cheeks burned with humiliation as she found herself begging this stranger to do unthinkable things to her body.

"Take the rest off, Katla," he ordered, his voice thick and gruff now.

She gasped when her hands and the fabric of her gown slid across her breasts; they felt heavy and tender beneath her touch. Katla tugged the gown until she could slide it over her shoulders and down her hips. Letting it fall to the floor, she stepped over it and then met his gaze.

Hunger. Unsatisfied hunger and lust shone there in the depths of his pale blue eyes. Her body reacted to it, shuddering and trembling and blossoming under the heat of his gaze. That place between her legs wept now, the deepest folds swelling and aching and waiting for his attentions. Other than with his eyes, he did not touch her.

"Sit on the bed now."

She was enjoying this, too. Allowing him to command and guide her to pleasure. When she wished, she lost herself and her will to it, and when she wished to be in command of her actions, she could do that, too. Like some potion or brew, his scent seemed to intoxicate her. Katla walked past him, noticing that his hands lifted as though to touch her, before he dropped them and simply watched her every move. When she got to the bed, she sat on the side of it as he'd commanded.

"Spread your legs wide for me, angel," he said.

He nearly lost his breath when she opened her legs, exposing the blond curls and the feminine folds between them to his gaze. His breathing grew shallow and fast. He was nearing the end of his ability to control his raging lust, but he would. Gavin then gave her an order he was not certain she would obey.

"Pleasure yourself."

He watched as confusion filled her face for a few moments,

and then she gave a smile that would have tempted Adam from Paradise. He held his breath, waiting to hear the sounds that her body would make as she touched herself.

She had not done this before. Her uncertain movements spoke of her inexperience, and his own desire urged him to help. He walked over to her and knelt between her legs. When she stopped, probably believing he would do it for her, he laughed.

"Like this, Katla," he said, guiding her fingers to the wetness in the depths of her womanly channel and sliding the moisture over the folds to ease her path. "Touch here."

Gavin spread her nether lips and placed her fingers on the bud that lay at the center of her sensitivity. As she began to explore her body and seek a way to gain pleasure from her own touch, he lifted her legs, one at a time, removing her shoes and stockings and placing them so that her heels rested on the edge of the bed, giving him a better view of her most private parts. He heard her body begin to sing and knew she would come soon.

Katla had found a sensitive place and began to rub it in earnest, slower and faster, letting the shivers pass through her at each stroke. She discovered that using one hand to hold the folds of skin open and the other to stroke intensified the feelings. When she glanced at his face, she knew he was pleased. But still it was not enough. She could not do what he had done there and she wanted to feel the heat of his mouth bringing her to completion.

"Help me," she begged. "Help me."

She held out her hand, motioning to her body. Instead of his mouth, he reached out and thrust his middle fingers deep into her, using his thumb to stroke the fold from bud to opening. When she stopped her own movements, expecting him to finish it, he laughed and pulled her hand back there.

"Finish it, Katla. Find your pleasure."

As long as she touched, he did. As long as she stroked, he did. As long as she rubbed, he did. Her body tightened deep within, weeping even more, and he soon added a third finger to the other two that plunged inside her and stroked their way out. He pressed his thumb as he rubbed, and the feel of it, the pressure of it, made her throb even more. Her legs shook, but he leaned against them to steady them, never relinquishing his hold on her cleft.

Something snapped within her, and she leaned her head back and moaned as wave after wave of pleasure rolled over and through her. Her body arched against his hand, again and again, but he did not slow his pace. Never ceasing, never slowing, never letting up on the pressure of his thumb, he pushed her over some edge until she screamed out her release. Her body shook and trembled as pleasure pulsed through it.

"Sing, my angel, sing," he commanded, and her body arched and sang for him.

Gavin closed his eyes and felt the spasms around his fingers, the wetness as her release flowed, and he heard the song of her blood and her satisfaction. Against the utter silence in his head, it was a beautiful sound, one that he wanted to hear over and over.

Fearing that his release would bring an end to the pleasure and the silence, he fought the need to plunge his cock into her depth and spill his seed. He withdrew his hand and placed both palms on the bed on either side of her, panting and clenching his teeth against the nearly overwhelming urge to finish it now. He heard the deep exhalation of her lungs as her body relaxed from the intensity of her release and felt her legs slide off his chest and hang over the bedside.

Gavin was only waiting for her to recover before he sought his own pleasure. The silence calmed his raging spirit and eased the pain in his head and ears, and for a moment, he thought he could actually hear her breathing. Turning his head to face her, he realized the folly of such a thought when she spoke and the words did not penetrate his deafness after all.

Katla smiled at him and let out another breath before trying to sit up. She leaned up on her elbows and looked him over, from head to knees before shaking her head. The flush of her skin, the sparkle in her eyes, the becoming blush in her cheeks all told of a woman well sated, and it pleased him to know that she had found such pleasure with him. When she reclined so before him, his mouth watered once more, anxious for a taste of her skin and her arousal and those wonderful, full breasts with their enticing rosy tips.

If he thought his erection would ease, he was mistaken, for her presence and closeness and the musky smell of her release made him even harder. His cock tented out his trews, clearly visible in its rampant state to both of them. His body readied anew, throwing off more of the scent until her eyes clouded and her hips arched up as though in invitation.

He would have resisted, he could have resisted, until she pulled her legs up and turned onto her knees, offering her arse to him. His hands had the ties of his trews loosened and his cock freed in moments. It took only a few strokes to arouse her with his hands and fingers in her cleft. Like a female animal in heat, she offered herself higher and higher, rubbing against his hands and pressing against his groin until she was panting again.

She slid over his cock, spreading her moisture on him. Gavin gritted his teeth against the pleasure of it, reaching around to touch that sensitive bud from the front while she writhed against him, grinding the cheeks and cleft of her arse against his readied flesh. Grabbing his prick in one hand, he spread her cheeks and pressed against the puckered opening once and then again.

In spite of her body's movements and enticement, he realized she was untried there, so he slid lower and found the opening to her woman's channel. There would be time and opportunity to initiate her in the pleasures of the other one soon enough. Right now, his cock felt ready to spill his seed, so he plunged in as deeply as he could, seating himself with ease until his sac touched the curls of her mons.

Katla arched against him then, grinding her buttocks against his groin, urging him in deeper still. Using her hands to steady herself, she clenched the muscles deep within her channel to hold him tightly. His cock moved with ease and when he moved, he withdrew and then thrust, hitting her womb. She tightened again, clenching his hardness within her, and he laughed. He withdrew, angled his hips differently, and then plunged in again, this time sliding along another part of that place which caused a shivering friction.

She could not explain the urge she'd had to turn onto her knees and offer him her bottom because she'd never been taken from behind. But she followed her body's urgings and discovered the excitement of such a position. She could not see his face or tell what he was going to do, and the anticipation increased her pleasure. Even the first tentative movements against her bottom had thrilled, not frightened, her.

Katla felt his hands on her hips, pulling her back and up, so she moved on her knees until she could lift herself higher for him. When his hand encircled her and teased the still-aching bud between her legs, she dropped her head and keened out at the sensations. It spurred her body on, seeking that satisfaction she'd found just minutes earlier.

Her muscles screamed out with tension; something wound tighter and tighter within her until she felt his prick lengthen and grow harder in her core. When he thrust in and filled her, she felt the walls holding him spasm and throb, and another release overwhelmed her. The hot bursts of his seed spilling and the moisture of her own second release mixed until even her womb vibrated as her body peaked with his.

Katla held her body against his as he finished, and then they both fell to the bed. He put his arm around her and pulled her against him, his prick still pulsing at the mouth of her womb. She gasped at every movement, her skin sensitive to any touch now. It took a while for their bodies, their racing hearts, their labored breathing and pulsing blood to calm. He was still hard within her as she drifted off to an exhausted sleep.

She woke up in the dark of night to find him exploring her body once more. Somehow he'd managed to remove his tunic and trews without moving from his place behind her. Once again, his cock was lodged deep within her. His hands teased her breasts and tickled her skin until she writhed against his hard, hot body. He slowed his movements and turned the bout of bedplay into something quiet and tantalizing.

Every slide of his prick, every caress, every kiss happened as though they had all the time in the world and all the control in the world, too. And he seemed to. Knowing what awaited her at the end made Katla anxious to reach it, but he soothed her and gentled her under a steady hand. When she tried to hasten her pleasure as he'd shown her earlier, he held her hands above her head and continued his maddeningly slow pace.

She pleaded with him. She begged him. She promised any number of things, but all the while he moved from one throbbing, aching pleasure point to the next. No words would sway him from whatever course of seduction he'd set.

When he reached the moment when he decided to end it, he moved like the fury of a winter storm over her, full of breathtaking caresses and unmatched passion until they both screamed out their release.

Completely satiated and exhausted from their bouts of loveplay, Katla lacked the strength to move. The lethargy robbed her of the ability or the will to leave his bed. As she fell into a deep sleep, one question plagued her.

How many times could he couple with her in one night and still want more?

Chapter Eight

Gavin watched her sleep, afraid to fall into the clutches of that state himself. Hour after hour, he waited for the voices to return, but each time he coupled with Katla his ability to push them away seemed stronger. And he'd coupled with her five times during the night.

He'd told himself it was simple lust. He'd told himself it was curiosity. He'd told himself many things through that night, but each time he spilled his seed within her, he wanted her more. If she'd been slow to arouse or not willing, he would have stopped, but each time he stroked her body or kissed her mouth or skin, she responded with a full measure of passion that he could not resist or refuse.

Each time.

He chuckled then, knowing he was not being completely honest.

He wanted her for more than the way he felt while wrapped around her in passion's play. He wanted her for the complete silence that she seemed to create within his tumultuous mind.

Complete.

At peace.

Silent.

Now, as the rising sun's light began to creep into his chambers, he swore he would not swive her again as long as she did not ask him to. He could resist the nearness of her warm and lush body if he had to. He could even understand if she refused. She moved then, turning to him in her sleep and murmuring something he thought he could almost hear, and he was hard again.

Gavin listened, trying to discern whether his ears could hear yet, and trying to ignore the very real call of her body to his. When her hand touched his cock, it twitched to life once more. When her hand encircled his hardness and began to slowly move her fingers up and down the length of it, he met her gaze and knew it was an invitation and not an accidental touch. He lay there, letting her stroke him for as long as he could resist and then rolled over on her, spreading her legs with his and easing right inside her. She gasped as he filled her, arching her back and hips and pulling him in deep, then letting out a soft sigh.

He heard the sounds inside his mind, but also faintly with his ears.

"Have I hurt you, Katla?" he asked her, now starting to hear her words. The deafness had lasted for nigh on four days this time, longer than the previous two months.

"I am sore, but do not stop now," she said, her voice hoarse as though she'd been shouting too much. He smiled then, for he knew she'd screamed out her release each time she'd reached it and that had been more times than he had. Yes, he knew her throat also must be sore.

"Then I will do as you bid, lady," he said, kissing her neck and then her mouth.

Gavin took his time, moving in and out of her in easy strokes, not too fast or hard or deep, and not too slow. She moved her hips in rhythm with his, not taking him in as deeply as she had during the night, but still bringing him indescribable pleasure. She did not disappoint him, giving full measure of herself and not reaching her peak until he was ready as well.

This time he could hear the sounds of her body and their cries as they echoed through the chamber. Better, he could hear the sound of her voice as she whispered his name over and over again while the passion subsided in her body.

And nothing else.

Gavin listened again. Nothing.

No thoughts that were not his. No sounds racing through his mind that were not those made by Katla's body as she blossomed with desire or reached satisfaction. He laughed then, not understanding the silence at all and not willing to jeopardize it by questioning how it happened or why. Rolling off her and pulling her into his arms, he kissed her once more.

"Do I amuse you?" she asked, pulling the bedcovers free of their tangled bodies and straightening them.

" 'Tis not you, Katla, but my circumstances that I laugh at," he replied. "Something has changed, and I know not the why or how of it."

He did seem a different person this morn. Last evening, he'd shouted at people who were not there, sounding and appearing mad. She'd witnessed similar behavior when she'd spied on him in the cave. Bouts of uncontrolled rage, shouting, screaming about the pain and noises in his head. She'd watched him consume huge amounts of spirits and healers' potions. And all of it unsuccessful until now.

This morn, he seemed at peace with himself. He did not call out to others not present. He did not writhe in pain and demand ale or other intoxicants. He did not seem like some otherworldly truthsayer with powers that others did not possess—he seemed like any other man.

Something *had* changed.

The door to his chambers opened, interrupting whatever he

wanted to say to her, and Haakon entered. The Truthsayer did not seemed surprised by his servant's arrival, but the man stopped and stared, his mouth gaping open, clearly not able to speak whatever words he'd been about to say.

"Good morrow, Haakon," the Truthsayer called out to his servant. She watched in silence as he climbed from the bed and accepted the cup his shocked servant held out to him. Unmindful of his nakedness, he drank from it while he walked to the door and opened it to look out on the water.

"Call for a bath and a meal for us," he said without looking back at either of them.

Haakon rushed over, handed him a small, wrapped bundle and whispered something she could not hear. His master, and hers for the next month, spoke softly in reply, too softly for her to hear. She waited for their disagreement to be resolved so that she could get out of bed.

The conversation ended with Haakon leaving the room, a sour expression on his face. He did not glance at the bed or acknowledge her in any way. The door slammed loudly and she winced at the noise.

"Haakon is not happy," she said, pushing the covers back and slipping from the bed. The cold of the floor against her bare feet chilled her and gooseflesh broke out on her skin.

Katla walked over to where her garments lay on the floor and picked them up. She turned, shaking them out, and met his gaze. The intensity of his eyes, the desire there, made her shiver. Her first impulse was to cover herself, but the way he stared at her body made her not wish to do so. No one had ever looked on her with such passion, so she stood unmoving as his eyes roamed over her skin in a way that felt as though he touched her in every place his gaze did. Then the Truthsayer approached, holding out the bundle that Haakon had brought into the room.

"For you," he said in a husky voice that echoed the arousal his body already demonstrated. Katla forced herself to take the bundle, though her body urged her to toss it aside and take his cock in her hands instead.

Untying the string and peeling back the cloth, she discovered a breathtaking pair of armbands, carved with intricate patterns and inlaid with jewels of varying colors. She held them up and examined them. 'Twas only then that she noticed the matching neck ring still in the cloth. Stunned by the value of the pieces and by their beauty, she gasped and then shook her head.

"I cannot accept such things from you, Truthsayer." Katla wrapped the cloth around the splendid pieces and held them out to him. "I cannot."

Such jewelry was given to a woman held in high esteem. Such adornments cost a fortune to commission from the goldsmith and the jeweler. Such gifts turned what had happened between them into something less honorable than a quest to save her brother's life—it turned her into a whore. She shook her head again and pushed the bundle into his hands.

"I cannot," she repeated.

He walked to her, naked and rampant again, and took the jewelry from her. But instead of taking it away, he held the pieces up before him.

"These are gifts, nothing more, nothing less," he said. His voice was pitched low, and the sound of it flowed over her like a warm shower.

Her good sense told her to refuse, but his next words made it impossible to do that.

"It would please me if you wore them."

She told herself that she must please him if she expected his help determining Kali's fate, but that was not the reason he had the power to draw her into his web of desire and pleasure.

She told herself that she could resist. But in only hours and a handful of encounters, he'd trained her body to his touch and it responded. She allowed him to do it once more.

He did not wait for further excuses or refusals, he simply slid on one of the arm rings, positioning it and caressing her breast with the back of his hand as he did. She trembled. When he did the same with the other one, she tried to fight her response, but her legs shook in anticipation. Even knowing that the slight brush of his hand against the sensitive skin of her breasts was done apurpose did not lessen its effect on her.

Only the neck ring was left in his grasp, and she closed her eyes as he drew nearer still and gathered her hair, lifting it away from her shoulders and neck so he could place the piece there. The heat of his skin nearly burned hers as he brushed against her. He moved to stand behind her, his hands still touching her shoulders and neck, caressing them as he locked the neck ring and then kissing her just above where it lay.

He moved his mouth around her throat, using the jeweled collar as a guide, kissing and nipping the skin until she panted. His erect cock pressed into her hip and her back as he made his way around her body and he rubbed it against her, mimicking the way he'd rocked it deep inside her flesh all those times.

This man had taken her body five or six times throughout the night, so many that she'd lost count of them. Now, in the light of day, he continued his sensual pursuit of pleasure and showed no signs of slowing down or losing interest in her body. Did he mean to take her again?

He encircled her with his arms then, holding her tightly against him, and heat pulsed through her. With one arm over her breasts and the other sloping across her stomach to her legs, he controlled her every movement. Katla leaned her head back against his chest and let him.

She found herself holding her breath as his fingers moved in light, small circles, teasing her skin and making her want to beg him to hurry as he touched his way to the curls between her legs. With his hand splayed wide over the curls, one of his fingers dipped into the already-aching cleft, making her moan and open her legs to him. About to give herself over to the full pursuit of pleasure, Katla heard a sound she could not identify and opened her eyes.

Harald Erlendson stood at the door of the chamber, staring at them. Katla had not heard the door open, but from the way his eyes flashed and his lips thinned, she knew he'd seen too much. Though his hand went to the sword at his side, he stopped and turned away. No words came to her mind that she could say to him. It mattered not because before she could loosen herself from the Truthsayer's embrace, Harald disappeared.

Chapter Nine

Complete and utter rage boiled over from inside him, and Harald knocked down any number of people in his way when he left Gavin's chamber. His heart pounded in his chest, and his eyes burned as he made his way out of the earl's house. Pushing through those working or walking in the yard, he sought the training field, knowing he could batter and battle other warriors to burn out his sudden need to kill.

Gavin the Truthsayer should die.

The smell of spent seed and a night of sexual excess burned his nostrils, and he tried to breathe in the fresh, cold air as he walked. But any attempts to calm himself or to blunt the rage eating him from the inside out failed. If any of the men realized the cause of his fury, they did not speak of it. A good thing, for death would be his reply.

Harald tore off his tunic and drew his sword, calling out insults and a challenge to all present. Within seconds it seemed, nearly a dozen men answered and he was attacked from all sides. He held his ground while offering a punishing assault to anyone who got too close. When he lost his sword some time later, he pummeled with his fists and feet. But even when he

was beaten to the ground and too exhausted and too hurt to
rise, the rage yet swirled in his gut.

The image of Katla being pleasured by another man still
burned bright in his memory. Worse, he had called Gavin
"friend."

He could hear the sounds of her excited breathing. He saw
the flush of passion on her skin. He remembered the sight of
Gavin's hand between her legs, claiming something that
should be Harald's alone. He screamed out his rage to the sky,
not caring in that moment who witnessed his fury.

The others left him where he lay, not speaking a word and
never admitting that everyone within the earl's household
knew where and how his woman had spent the night. But to a
one, they also understood that no one, not even Harald, had
the power to stop it. So valuable to the earl was the Truthsayer
that anyone denying a request from him risked dire punishment. When his breathing had slowed, Harald struggled to his
feet. He thought several ribs might be broken. He bled from
several gashes on his face. He spit out a mouthful of blood and
used his tongue to feel for loosened teeth. Pushing his mud-
died hair from his face, he walked out of the yard toward the
water's edge. A boy caught up with him and, without a word,
handed him his tunic and his sword.

When he reached the shoreline, he stopped only to remove
his boots. Dropping his sword and tunic on the sand next to
them, he walked into the bay. Once the cold had soaked
through his trews, he tugged them off. He dunked his head
under the surface a few times to loosen all the caked-in mud.

Harald splashed his face and used his hands to get rid of the
blood there. He'd hope that the cold water would cool the
rage that seethed inside him, but it did nothing. No matter
how hard he pushed away the memories, they returned anew.

He'd been present for the Truthsayer's rituals and had

served as his bodyguard a dozen or more times since Gavin had joined the earl's household. Harald knew his ways. He only kept a woman for a few hours, never longer, because he exhausted them with his lust. He never called married women or those belonging to other men to his bed. If they came to him anyway, he sent them away untouched.

He'd broken all those rules when he'd summoned Katla to him last night. Now, when he closed his eyes, Harald did not see Katla during one of the dozens of times he'd bedded her. Nay, now the only thing he could see was the way she'd looked in the Truthsayer's arms. Her mouth had dropped open as he stroked her, and she writhed against his naked body. Worse, she wore naught but expensive gold and bejeweled armbands and neck rings that he could never afford to give to her.

And neither one even noticed him standing before them.

He pounded his fists on the surface of the water, sending out waves in all directions and splashing himself with an icy shower. Dunking his head once more, he realized that the worst part of this was that Katla had never made a sound during their coupling.

At first, after taking her as his second wife in the old tradition, he'd gone to her bed and tried to be as quick and easy as he could. Harald understood that she only offered herself to him to save her brother, but it did not mean that he did not have feelings for her. Oh, aye, lust was one of them, for she was a beautiful young woman and he had the appetite of a man. So, he took her maidenhead with care and swived her quickly when he sought her bed.

Regardless of her apparent lack of feelings for him, he found himself there many nights each week, bedding her almost to the exclusion of his wife and other mistress. He wanted to make her want him, he wanted her to be happy with him, and he wanted to take the ever-present sadness from her eyes. When she did not show enthusiasm or desire in their bed, he accepted it and did not dally there, expecting bedplay she did not want or a passion she did not feel. From the sounds that escaped Gavin's chambers and echoed throughout the earl's house in the silence of the night, Katla was definitely capable of feeling passion, but not for him. He pounded the water again at the realization that the Truthsayer had the woman he wanted and had somehow unleashed the desire within her that Harald wanted for himself.

He walked out of the water and sluiced off what he could. Tugging his tunic over his head, he made his way back to his chamber to change his clothing and see to his duties. And it was then that Harald realized the true problem at the heart of his rage and jealousy.

He had fallen in love with Katla Svensdottir.

The thought stopped him. Pushing his sodden hair away from his face and wringing out as much water as he could, he fought the truth. He wanted her, surely, for he had watched her grow from a young girl to a beautiful woman, full of life and intelligence. He desired the woman she'd become.

But in the months since her father had tried to draw him into the plot to rid Orkney of the earl and into the plot that extended to the Scots kingdom in order to gain importance in the eyes of the king, she'd become something more important to him.

He'd seen the way she organized and controlled her father's household with a quick wit and an efficient hand. Witnessed her strong and honorable behavior when her father was arrested and as she challenged him in order to save her brother. Seen the way she fulfilled her part of their bargain, never acting as though it was anything but her idea to be in his bed.

All those things had made him fall in love with her. And

even knowing that she did not love him in return and never would if she learned the extent of his involvement in her father's demise did not lessen his growing need for her. He laughed harshly then—the irony of the situation was not lost on him at all.

Both he and Gavin pursued her for their own reasons: his was love, Gavin's was lust. He suspected that in the end, neither would end up with Katla or deserve her if they did.

Harald walked down the corridor to his chambers, not meeting the gaze of anyone he passed. His feelings were too close to the surface, and he feared his temper was not yet under control. Let the others veer from his path and give him some time to accept the situation. He needed to be rid of this rage before Katla returned to him tonight.

Above all, he needed to banish the image of the two of them, naked, entwined in passion. Taking a deep breath, he turned the corner and watched as one of the servants left his room. Good. He wanted no one rushing around his chambers now. He wanted to see and speak to no one for a while. Lifting the latch on his door, he pushed it open and walked inside.

Katla sat in the chair in the corner, watching him with a different emotion from the sadness that usually shone within. Now it was fear he saw, and it turned his stomach.

He looked terrible.

One side of his jaw was swollen and he bled from two cuts on his cheek and forehead. He limped into the room, favoring his left leg. Harald wore only his tunic and carried his boots, trews, belt and sword.

And it was her fault.

Standing, she went to him and took his clothing and sword, placing them on the table. Pointing at the chair, she nodded to him.

"Sit, Harald. Let me see to your injuries."

Katla poured some water from the pitcher into the wash-basin and dipped a cloth in it. Dabbing it on the cuts she found on his face and scalp, moving his hair aside to check for more, she finally stopped most of the bleeding. None of the gashes she saw would require stitching.

She was used to treating injuries and illnesses in her father's household and used to treating those of headstrong, belligerent men, so she did not ask his permission to do what she did—she simply went ahead and cleaned and bandaged him. She heard his indrawn breath a few times, once as she wrapped some lengths of cloth around his chest to support his bruised ribs, and once when she leaned over and her breasts rubbed against his back.

He was too proud to mention the reason for his injuries, but Haakon had come and reported back to the Truthsayer when he'd sent his servant to follow Harald. Katla had dressed and left the Truthsayer's chambers, but could not catch up with Harald. She watched from a hidden corner as he walked onto the training field and taunted those there into fighting him. Her stomach clenched and tears burned her throat and eyes as he was pummeled into the ground.

Because of her.

Katla returned to his chambers to wait for him, knowing the worst was yet to come. For unlike the dozens or hundreds of other women before her, the Truthsayer had not tired of her. He'd told her that there was something different about her and that he needed her to come back to Durness with him until the next full moon. And he'd promised to hear her brother's truth at the next ritual.

Harald would never understand or forgive her now. Chances were that once the Truthsayer tired of her, Harald would not take her back.

She would never forget the expression in his eyes when their gazes met. Shock and hurt showed clearly there, as well as anger and jealousy. But the worst was the disappointment she read in his eyes. When her father gave her the same look, it was a more effective punishment than any beatings or deprivations, for she'd always wanted to prove herself to him and never had.

After Katla finished seeing to Harald's injuries, she handed him a cup of beer and waited for him to drink it down. The healer had sent over some herbs that would help the pain he was surely feeling. She cleaned up the basin and waited, trying to think of a way to tell him Gavin's new request.

"My thanks for your care," Harald said in his gruff voice. He stood, but he wobbled on his feet. "With the earl gone, I have not trained in a long time." His excuse went unchallenged, for she knew him to be a proud man.

"Harald," she said as she sat on a stool near him, "there is more you must know."

The Truthsayer had said that no one would know until she'd told Harald, and he had offered to tell him for her but she needed to do this. She clasped her hands in her lap and met Harald's gaze. He'd emptied it of any indication of what he felt, so she could not tell what his reaction would be.

"He has asked me to go to Durness with him until the next full moon in exchange for helping Kali. I agreed."

His response was . . . nothing. Other than a quick inhalation, Harald did nothing and said nothing for a full minute. Then he stood, walked to the trunk that held his clothing, and finished dressing before facing her.

"And this is your decision? Not his will imposed on you?" he asked, staring at her.

"Aye. I am not under his power now, Harald. For Kali, I must—" He interrupted before she could finish.

"Play his whore for a month, Katla? How does this honor

your father or your brother when their reputation must be bought by your dishonor?" He crossed his arms over his chest and shook his head. "Your father would have had you whipped to within an inch of your life and thrown you out. Your brother, if he is proven innocent of your father's machinations, will be humiliated at the price."

A man speaking of the way men looked at honor. She let out a breath. "But he will be alive, will he not? And he can learn to accept the price I paid."

"You stand to lose much more doing this than you have lost already. Do you understand that?" he asked.

She stood, walked to him, and laid her hand on his chest.

"I cannot let my brother die if there is something I can do to stop it," she said softly.

"And letting the Truthsayer use your body is no hardship for you, is it?"

Her first reaction was anger at his insult; then guilt slapped her at his accusation. A good woman would not sink to whoring as she had done. A good woman would accept that men would handle matters of honor. A good woman would beg for Harald's forgiveness and refuse the Truthsayer's scandalous demand. And though she did not consider herself a good woman any longer, she would not give false reasons, not even in her own mind.

"Nay, Harald. 'Tis no hardship."

He looked away from her and then stepped back, as though her touch was something to be avoided. It would have been easier to pretend she was facing something too horrible to bear, but Harald deserved more than that.

"And when the full moon comes again?" From the even tone he used, she could not tell if he was hoping for a life with her or hoping to avoid it now.

"After Kali is freed, we will have many things to discuss."

It was all she could say, for she had no idea what her future would hold. If Kali was humiliated by the price she paid . . . well, that was something she would have to deal with when it happened.

"What will you do, Harald? Would you even consider offering me a place in your household then?"

Katla braced herself for the answer, knowing in her heart he would not, could not, make such an offer. Harald did not reply; he stood searching her face as though he sought the answer there.

"When do you leave?" he asked instead of answering.

She shrugged. "I know not. He wanted to do nothing until you were told." She paused then, knowing that her next suggestion was a strange one. But it would give Harald a way in which to salvage some of his pride.

"I think you should turn me out of your household."

Harald frowned at her words. "What?"

"If you publicly disavow me, your honor will not suffer because of my choice."

It seemed straightforward to her—if it was known he'd turned his back on her this day, he would appear to be protecting his honor and would not suffer humiliation from her acts. In her mind, it was one way to prevent him further problems. Katla watched as his expression hardened and he shook his head.

Without a word, he turned and left the room, slamming the door behind him. Unsure whether she should return to the Truthsayer's chambers or wait for him to summon her, Katla decided to wait. Knowing that she would have to pack, she found a servant in the corridor and asked her to find Godrod. She also asked if the woman knew where Harald had headed.

When the woman pointed in the direction of the Truthsayer's chambers, Katla feared for both men. For Harald because the Truthsayer was high in the earl's esteem and could ruin him with a word. And for the Truthsayer because Harald was more dangerous when quiet and deliberate than when filled with rage.

Katla closed the door behind her and went to the Truthsayer's chambers, hoping to intervene before someone was hurt.

Chapter Ten

Gavin paced, feeling nervousness and anticipation growing within him. He'd never expected her to share herself with him so completely, never expected her to agree to accompany him back to Durness. Something wonderful happened when they joined: she made it possible for him to quiet the raging clamor in his head, even to block out the noise entirely.

With some time alone, he hoped to discover the reason for this new relief and to learn how to control the power that directed his life. For the first time since his power and its after-effects began to spin out of control, he dared hope that he might discover more information about his origins.

The footsteps approaching his door were moving fast and were too heavy to be a woman's. Haakon was in his bed-chamber preparing to leave, so it could not be him. There was only one, other than the earl, who would enter without arranging it beforehand. Harald barely stopped as he opened the door and then strode forward until he stood in front of Gavin. They had a friendship of a sort, one that would be sorely tested by the woman they both wanted.

The strange glint in his eyes should have been a warning to

Gavin, but his friend was usually not one stirred to violence. The punch landed on his jaw and drove him to his knees. Haakon heard and called out to the guards, but Gavin waved them all off. He and Harald would have this out man to man, friend to friend.

"Damn you! Why her?" he said. "Of all the women Magnus could provide, why must you have her?"

Gavin wiped his bleeding mouth with the back of his hand, not bothering to rise. "I have no choice, Harald." And he did not, for she was the first woman to give him peace. "The bigger question is why did you not tell her?"

"Tell her what?" he asked.

"That you love her."

Harald backhanded him then, and Gavin fell back onto the floor. "After what you have done and plan to do, do not tell me how I feel about her."

"If she'd known, mayhap she would not have sought me in Durness and ended up in my bed the first time. Have you thought of that?" he asked, knowing he was inviting more punishment, yet even more certain that this must be clear between them.

Harald glanced at him with bleak eyes and nodded. "Words are not something that spring easily to my tongue, *Truthsayer*. I offered her what she needed, believing that when she recovered from her sorrow, she would understand what I'd done. I hoped there would be time for words."

Harald reached down and helped him to his feet.

"Do not do this, Gavin. It will destroy her. You will finish with her and turn to others, and she will not understand."

"And she understands your having a wife before her?" Gavin asked. He wiped his mouth again. The look in Harald's eyes made him take a step back, out of reach.

"I offered her an honorable place in my household. She will be an important part of it. She could have a family and a good life with me. Katla understands that." Harald rubbed his ribs, and Gavin was reminded of the scene in the yard that no one knew he'd witnessed. "What do you offer her, other than a month of pleasure?"

Gavin lifted his hands and made fists, about to punch his friend, until he realized the man spoke the truth. And more of it than Harald knew or understood at this point. He dropped his hands.

"I need her, Harald. I need the peace and silence that her passion seems to bring to my soul." He shrugged, not knowing how to explain the weaknesses he'd hidden from everyone around him. "And I suspect I will have nothing to offer her when this is all done."

Harald searched Gavin's face.

"What do you mean? You have wealth beyond imagination. You have a high place in the earl's household and in his regard. What woman would not want that?" He thought on the gold neck ring and armbands Katla had worn this morning. Few men he knew could gift that kind of jewelry to their women.

He could tell Gavin was not certain how to explain what was bothering him. Over the years since the earl had found the Truthsayer, Gavin had never taken on airs or behaved as though he was better than anyone else. Indeed, until these last six or seven months when he'd begun to seek isolation in Durness, he'd trained with the other men, worked when needed, and been part of gatherings in Birsay.

But the last months had seen a staggering increase in his drinking and his strange and secretive behaviors. Gavin had begun to act like a madman at times. Sullen and silent at others.

The women had always been drawn to him—the attraction was part of his powers mayhap—but now his incessant need for them grew each month. He used them and discarded them. Until today. Until Katla.

Gavin sighed and met his gaze. "My powers are building toward some conclusion that I cannot know, but I fear it will mean the end of me."

Harald was stunned by this news. "Does the earl know?"

"'Tis not something I trust to a messenger. Since he has been away with the king in the Western Isles, we've had no discussion."

Harald shook his head. "Mayhap you misunderstand the signs? Mayhap this is leading to even more power? Is there no one who has knowledge of this?"

But Harald knew there was no such person. He'd been the one to seek out information about this man with the strange ability, like the soothsayers of legend. Though everything pointed back to Durness, the trail ended there, for the people who'd raised him had died years before and had never spoken of his origins.

"Nay." Gavin's voice was stark with fear.

But then Harald watched his eyes brighten as he gazed at something over his shoulder. He did not need to turn to see who stood there. "Do not hurt her, Gavin."

His friend nodded without looking away from her. Harald could hear her shallow breathing, as though she was out of breath from running. Bitterly, he wondered which of them she was worried over. "And do not disappoint her."

"Disappoint her?"

"She expects you to save her brother. That is why she will be your whore for the next month. It's why I let her search for a way to help him."

Gavin looked abruptly away from Katla and met his gaze. "Save her brother? That is what she asked me to do?"

"Aye. What did you think?" Harald realized just then that Gavin did not know the reason for Katla's agreement or the price he must pay. "How could you not know?"

Gavin grabbed his arm and drew him closer. Leaning in, he

spoke in a low tone so that none would hear. "After the ritual, I hear many voices, but not with my ears. They are deaf for days. If she asked that, I did not hear it." He glanced at her once more. "I thought she asked for something for you."

"I know not what demons ride your soul now, but do not make her part of it. If you cannot help her brother, do not let her believe you can. It is the only thing important to her now."

Harald stepped back from him and began to turn to leave. He must speak to Katla, and he steeled himself for the sight of her, pining for Gavin instead of him.

"She will need you, Harald. Say the words so she knows you will be there for her."

What a strange situation to be in, Harald thought. The two of them, both wanting the same woman, both unwilling to allow her to be hurt, both having been involved in the worst thing ever to happen to her. The two of them friends, unwilling to hurt each other. And all three using the others for their own reasons. How could this turn out well?

"She will damn us both for the parts we have played in destroying her family if she finds out the whole of it," he warned. "She knows I carried out the orders to bring her father to justice, but has no idea that we provided the reasons for such action on the earl's part."

Harald turned then, finished with words, and walked to the door of the chamber, where Katla did indeed stand waiting. But, instead of gazing at Gavin, she frowned and watched Harald approach with worry and concern in her eyes. She placed her hand on his arm when he came close enough.

"Are you well?" she asked, searching his face as though expecting more injuries.

"I will send your things to you," he replied, unable to say anything more personal.

"Harald . . ." she began. But she did not go on.

"Send me word if you need me," he offered. "Protect yourself, Katla. Do not let your heart be involved in this . . . arrangement. He will only break it."

He watched as her lips trembled and her hands shook. Harald kissed her on the forehead and left her to his friend.

Chapter Eleven

After days of wondering whether his angel was real and then an entire night of unbridled pleasure with her, Gavin finally accepted that she was indeed made of flesh and blood. After making a hasty departure from Birsay, they'd set up camp en route to Durness. Now an awkward silence fell between them. He did not know what to do next.

And he would have her for a whole month.

As his exhausted body reminded him, they could not couple every minute of every day of the next thirty or so days. There needed to be something else between them. Growing to manhood, he'd often dreamed of having a family, but when his gift became apparent, so, too, did his need and attraction for women.

At first, it manifested itself as simply an ability to draw women to him and into his bed. As the strength of his powers grew, so did his sexual hunger and the ability to actually draw or summon women to him. Then, that scent seemed to ensorcell them, bending them to his will.

Until now.

Until Katla.

His skills at bedplay were impressive, but they did not extend to his being at ease with women out of his bed. Truly, when he'd asked her to come back to Durness with him, he'd not thought of much other than bedding her. But now there would be time enough for other things. Like meals and walks and bedding her at leisure without the clamoring in his head or the insatiable need in his blood.

Though he expected the blur of thoughts and voices to begin again at any moment, he did seem able to push them away now. He pictured a wall in his mind and pushed the sounds behind it. Without the clatter, there was no pain. Without the pain, there was no need to drink himself insensible. Without the extended periods of drunkenness and unconsciousness, he could have a life.

He glanced across the tent to where she sat, silently folding her garments in the light of the oil lamp. Did she know her power? Did she know the extent of his? He had the next month to discover whatever linked them before he must return her to Harald.

He rubbed his jaw, sore where Harald had struck him, and considered his friend's actions. He would be far worse off if Harald had wanted him to be—he'd seen the powerful warrior in battle and in training, and Gavin knew he would still be facedown on the floor if Harald had intended it to be so.

No matter what Harald had said to either of them, Gavin knew his friend would take her back. Gavin had not realized what was between the two of them when he'd recognized Katla and ordered her brought to him. He'd given the order to Harald because Harald did his bidding. It was only when Katla arrived in his chambers and he saw the exchange of glances between them that he'd suspected an involvement.

Do not hurt her, Gavin. Harald's voice had spoken of his true feelings for Katla. Gavin recognized the love in his tone even if Harald had not.

A pang of guilt pierced him then, for he did not want to hurt either of them. But his actions had. His desperate desire to find answers, to find peace, and to find a balance to his life drove him. He would push aside his guilt.

Katla shifted then, sorting the clothing in the sacks her servant had brought to her after Harald left. It appeared to be everything she had, and it had been stuffed into the canvas sack in haste. He was content then to simply watch her—studying her movements.

They'd left as the tide returned, heading west and then south down the coast of the mainland. The weather had turned bad, and they were forced to land on the southern coast of Hoy, not daring to test the waters of the Pentland Firth. The voyage back to Durness would take longer than the one to Birsay, for they would be sailing against the currents much of the way and relying on rowers rather than the power of the wind. Gavin did not mind the rough seas, but he noticed that the color in Katla's face drained with each pitch and yaw of the boat.

When the suggestion was made to make camp on land, it had seemed a good idea to everyone. As the setting sun took refuge behind tumultuous clouds, they'd put up some tents and managed to cook a meal. By the time they'd eaten, it was pouring rain and they sought shelter inside for the night.

Katla had been quiet through the rest of the day, not speaking unless he spoke to her. Gavin found it strange to be with a woman in a companionable silence and not be seducing her. And he discovered an almost shyness in her behavior—strange for a woman who had been as intimate as one could be with a man. And with a month of nights filled with all manner of pleasurable acts stretched out ahead of them, he found he did not feel such a rampant need to take her this night.

Truly, he was exhausted. He had slept only fitfully after the ritual, not at all the night before. When their bedding was laid and the tent tied closed against the rain, his eyes would not stay open. He slid down and opened his arms to her. She did not hesitate to join him there, putting out the lamp and climbing into the pile of blankets and furs. In moments she lay snuggled in his embrace as the rains beat against the canvas of the tent.

He had not even bothered to remove his clothing, and so he started out of a doze when he felt her untying the laces of his tunic. His placed his hand over hers.

"Nay, you do not have to do that," he whispered. The warmth of her nearness permeated his body, urging it to rest.

"I thought it was why you brought me with you," she answered, not moving her hand from beneath his.

He turned onto his side and pulled her next to him, spooning their bodies, and adjusted the furs over them. With only one good night's sleep in months, Gavin knew it would take many to feel restored.

"There will be time for everything else, Katla. For now, I just need to rest."

Katla listened as his breathing became deep and even and slow. He'd fallen asleep faster than she would have believed possible, and without one drink of wine or ale or other spirits as she knew was his usual habit. Haakon's face, and the surprise on it when the Truthsayer refused his offer of such, told her much about his dependence on those intoxicants.

His breath against her ear warmed and chilled her at the same time. She'd never slept the night with a man, so it was odd and uncomfortable in a way. Harald had always left her bed after coupling with her, never spending the night. Oh, she'd shared a bed or pallet with other women in her father's household when guests stayed or when her cousins came to visit. But to be held by a man who'd touched and pleasured every inch of her body . . . and who would again, caused a strange awareness within her.

A feeling that kept her awake most of the night in spite of the complete exhaustion in her body.

She dosed fitfully, unable to move much at all because his arm lying over her held her in place securely. Finally sometime deep in the dark of the night, she fell asleep.

"Katla."

His voice crept into the haze of sleep, but instead of waking her, she shifted against him and settled back to sleep.

"Katla," he repeated, this time squeezing her to rouse her. "We need to leave."

Katla pushed the hair back from her face and rubbed her eyes. Stretching out the stiffness in her arms and legs from remaining in one position too long, she rolled away from him and watched as he did the same. Sitting up, she rearranged her gown and tunic before standing. Being careful not to bang her head into the top of the tent, she crept to the open flap and climbed out.

The men were all busy about various tasks in their camp. The storm had blown past, and the day dawned crisp and clear and perfect for sailing. Some of the men were already loading their supplies back into the boat. One of the men handed her a bowl of some kind of porridge and a cup of watered ale as he passed. Haakon and two others emptied the Truthsayer's tent and took it apart, rolling the canvas around the short poles and storing it.

As she watched, the camp was dismantled, packed up, and readied for travel south. Katla felt lost, for she knew not her place here. Last night Gavin had rebuffed her touch, when she'd thought that was the reason he'd brought her along. Then this morning, he'd not acted on the arousal she could feel against her back when he woke her. Now, he was nowhere to be seen and she was left with the men. She found a place to sit and finished the food and drink given to her.

"Katla," Gavin called out as he approached. "Come."

He held his hand out to her and she stood. The same man who'd brought her the food and drink took the empty bowl and cup from her, and she followed the Truthsayer along the shore and then away from the water. The path led over the rocky outcrop and into some trees. After a few minutes, he stopped and pointed to the left.

"You can see to your needs at the stream there," he said, nodding off the path. "I will wait for you here."

Truly, 'twas not why she'd thought he'd led her away from the others, but she was grateful that he was taking care of her. Katla spent only a few minutes, washing her face, braiding her hair, and seeing to her personal needs before walking back to where he waited. Still, she felt uneasy in his company, uncertain of her place with him. Surely the others on the voyage understood the nature of their involvement; they all seemed to know him well and be familiar with this voyage.

Within half an hour's time, they boarded the boat and continued their journey, this time without the constant rocking and rolling of the boat on rough seas. Haakon explained their route and the length of time it would take to travel back to Durness. A small sitting area had been arranged for her at one end of the boat, and mostly she stayed there.

She watched Gavin, trying to sort out what kind of man he was now. She'd seen the angry, drunken man in pain. She'd seen the sexual creature he became. She'd seen the other-worldly being who shared his body during the ritual of hearing the truth. But now, she seemed to see just a man.

He walked among the crew speaking to those rowing, and he even helped with the sails a time or two. He spoke at length with Haakon, and they spared her several glances during those conversations. He smiled more than she'd ever seen him do, and each time, the lightness of his expression and the lack of turmoil on his face made him appear much younger. He seemed almost carefree at those times, and she wondered over the change.

"You look weary, Katla."

She did not realize he'd approached, but he crouched down in front of her now. "Are you well?" he asked. She nodded.

"I did not sleep well," she admitted. The Truthsayer sat next to her and drew her close.

"Here now, lean against me and sleep a bit. We have hours of sailing ahead and nothing much to do."

There it was again—that carefree attitude and tone.

"You are different, Truthsayer."

"Why do you not call me by name, Katla? Everyone else calls me Gavin. Save you." He smiled at her, a wicked glimmer in his eyes. "Except one time yesterday morning when I heard you speak my name. Over and over," he said in a whisper that matched the wickedness of his smile.

She shivered for she remembered it well. He'd been seated deep within her flesh, rocking his hips, making her gasp with each movement until she screamed out his name and her pleasure.

"Say my name, Katla," he urged, his voice deepened by desire. Or the memory of it.

She met his gaze and obeyed his words. "Gavin."

"Good. Better," he said, smiling. "And, aye, I am different," he admitted. He lowered the shoulder nearest her and nodded to her. "Rest a while. We have time to talk once we get to Durness."

With the long summer days and the sun setting late, they had enough light to sail for hours. From what she'd heard, they'd arrive at the cave by nightfall. She gave in to her exhaustion and slept, resting against him and waking sometime later to find her body reclining with his.

Once more he saw to her needs, providing food and drink

and a chance to relieve herself with a measure of privacy. When the cliffs and promontories of the north coast loomed ever larger, he stood next to her at the side of the boat, not touching, but close enough that the sound of his voice teased her skin.

"Why did you agree?" he asked.

"To save my brother's life," she answered without hesitation. She thought she might need to remind herself of that reason in the weeks ahead.

"Are you having regrets already?"

She turned to look at him. "Regrets? Nay, Gavin. I will carry out my part of the bargain." His gaze was intense. "Why do you think that?"

"You have been quiet. You've not spoken more than a dozen words since we left Birsay. I thought that mayhap you want to change your decision."

She heard it there—fear lay beneath his words. What did he have to fear?

"I know not my place with you. In my father's house, I knew what to do, and most answered to me. In Harald's household, I had duties and knew what was expected of me. Now, I am here with you and do not know what you expect of me."

He surprised her by taking her hand in his and tugging her to face him.

"You are my guest, Katla. I want you to be comfortable during your stay. The rest we will take one step at a time."

She wanted to be clear about this, for he did not seem to have the same appetites of a day ago. "And I am to please you in whatever manner you ask."

He lifted her hand to his mouth and kissed the inside of her wrist. "It will be about *our* pleasure, Katla. We will seek it together."

"I do not understand, Gavin," she began. "Why did you ask me to come here with you, if not to serve you?"

He turned away and stared out toward their destination. Then he smiled.

"To save my life, Katla. Nothing more, nothing less."

Chapter Twelve

Gavin wondered if that was the answer he should have given. He'd believed her tied to his fate in some unexplainable way, but telling her that was not the best idea. Not until he'd been able to learn what she knew of him and his power and, more important, his origins or his end.

One of the men called, removing him from her side for a short time. When he glanced back, she was organizing their supplies and clothing. Then he helped the men during their arrival at the cave, and it felt good. For too long he'd been a prisoner of the noise in his thoughts, forced away from others because of the pain. Now here he was, with silence in his mind because of her.

Once they landed near the cave's entrance, the supplies were carried down the path and inside to be stored, under Haakon's direction. Afterward, the men boarded the boat to sail back to Durness village, a few miles west on the coast. They would stay there overnight, enjoying the hospitality the people offered. Some would visit family there before returning north. In a short time, Haakon excused himself, climbing to the small croft that he'd built on the ground above the cave.

By the time night fell, Gavin was alone with Katla.

She stood by the entrance to the cave, on the small beach there, staring up at the sky. Thousands of stars lit the clear night above them, and the sound of the sea lapping against the shore soothed him. 'Twas one of the reasons he'd sought refuge here. Now, he heard it with silence in the background of his thoughts and enjoyed it even more. Gavin walked up behind her and waited for her to notice him there, not wanting to invade her private thoughts. When she glanced back, he spoke.

"It is beautiful at night, is it not? The sides of the cliffs seem to draw the starlight between them."

"Aye," she said, turning to face him. "Is that what brought you here?"

"Nay. I only noticed it after I moved here." He smiled.

How could he explain to her the soothing effect of the rushing water from the river and the sea crashing on the beach? Would she decide that he was mad as others claimed?

"Did you see the whole cave when you were here?" he asked. He'd been drugged and remembered very little about her first visit, except the pleasure of the dreamlike experience.

"Nay," she said, shaking her head. "I thought you were asleep and did not want to be discovered spying on you," she explained, a soft pink blush creeping up her cheeks as she spoke of that time. He would ask her more about that later; for now he would play the gracious host.

"Come," he said, holding out his hand to her. "Let me show you the rest."

He took her hand and they walked along the edge of the river that led deeper into the cave. Crossing over a small bridge he'd had built, they entered the main area that lay open to the sea. Gavin took her into one of the side caves that led to the private area he used as a bedchamber. Sheltered deeper within the cave's inner recesses, it was not as damp or cold as the outer chamber where she'd first found him. He observed as she entered and looked around. The earl's men and wealth had turned it into a comfortable place—for a sea cave. The bed stood high off the floor, which lay covered in thick rugs. Furs were piled high on the bed, making it warm even during the colder nights. A metal brazier sat in one corner, where he could burn wood or peat to heat the room. The smoke followed the ceiling of the chamber and the corridor out. His trunks of clothing, a set of shelves with some books and supplies, a table and two chairs completed the furnishings—simple but comfortable.

"Is this the only chamber?" she asked.

"Aye. Haakon prefers to sleep above the ground in the croft there." She nodded, clearly knowing the existence and location of it. "But there is more to the cave."

Katla followed him as he retraced their path back to the main chamber, where he took a torch down from the wall and led her down a different corridor. This one narrowed as it moved along the river that drained through the cave into the sea. They walked in the light of the torch for a few minutes and then he stopped.

"Can you hear it?" he asked. They were very close to the waterfall, though they could not see it in the darkness.

She closed her eyes for a short time and then nodded. "Aye, the waterfall." When she opened her eyes, she laughed at him. "I did not simply enter your cave without first searching the area for an easier entrance."

"Did you not use the path in front? The way we entered?"

"Nay," she said. "I did not want to chance being seen on the open path, so I climbed down the cliff."

He choked back a gasp. She could have been killed by the fall from the cliffs. "Remind me to stay out of your path when you are determined to do something, Katla Svensdottir!" he said. Then he asked the question that had plagued him. "Why did you come here and leave without a word?"

She did not answer him right away, apparently picking and choosing her words before speaking. Then she sighed and told him.

"My task that day was to search your cave to learn more about you. I wanted to find out something I could use to convince you to help me . . ." Her words drifted off.

"Save your brother's life," he finished.

"Aye."

He offered his hand to her and led her back into the main chamber, then into his bedchamber before asking her more questions.

"Why are you the only one seeking to change his fate? Do you believe he is innocent just because he is your brother?"

From what Haakon had told him of Sven Rognvaldson and his son, it seemed that both were deeply involved in plotting against the earl, possibly with the Scots king. Now that there was a treaty between King Magnus and King Edgar, neither sovereign wanted to upset the tenuous peace between the two nations. Sven Rognvaldson had clearly had other plans and sought a way to garner more power and more importance to both kings.

"He *is* innocent!" she said sharply. It did not take a truthsayer to tell she was also trying to convince herself of her words. He could see how upset she was, so he took her in his arms and held her close.

"Hush now," he whispered. "I did not mean to upset you so."

They stood like that for several minutes before he asked another question.

"Why did Harald not help you?"

"He cannot go against the earl without proof," she explained. "Or appear to be disobeying the earl's orders in this matter. My father had many enemies, and they would rather see no one left alive to claim his properties and wealth. Harald gave me leave to find proof that he could use to raise questions to the earl."

Even as strong as she was, Katla's heart was the soft one of a woman. A woman who could not or would not see the failings in those she loved. But a woman who would hate someone who showed her those failings and forced her to see them. Harald clearly knew that, allowing her to seek the truth on her own so he would not be the one to prove her brother's involvement.

Especially not after being the one to accuse her father.

The earl had not believed Harald's claims of treason against the powerful chieftain, so he'd called on Gavin to determine the truth of the accusation.

As he had, though he remembered nothing of the words spoken by Harald during the ritual. Gavin never did. Many times he did not even know whose truth he heard. Though the earl's swift actions after the ritual told him everything he needed to know. Sven was guilty and Harald had spoken the truth. Magnus had carefully made his plans and set them in motion to rid himself of a traitor . . . and his son.

"So you believe him innocent then?"

She stepped back, out of his embrace, and he saw the tracks of tears on her cheeks. "Aye. I do." She nodded her head. "He is young, not yet fully a man," she explained. "He would never act with such dishonor."

Though Gavin could give her many examples of how her words were not accurate, including several children Kali Svenson had already fathered and other accusations made against him, he did not. He needed to understand her more fully, and her words revealed much about her character. Loyalty and love ran deep in her.

"This has been a long day. Do you need something to eat?" he asked. He walked over to the covered tray on the table, lifting the cover and showing her the food beneath it. "Haakon left us a meal if you are hungry."

She shook her head, an expression of wariness now filling her gaze.

"There is also ale or even wine, in these jugs here." He pointed to the containers on a shelf. "You are welcome to it."

He walked around the room, pointing out both the necessities and the luxuries, so that she would not feel ill at ease asking for this or that. Then when he'd completed the instructions, he found he was nervous. Anticipation of the night ahead rippled through him.

But the desperation to have her, to have any woman, was gone. Every month, once he recovered from the ritual and regained his hearing, he was struck by an overwhelming hunger for women. He coupled several times each day in that first week after the full moon, no more able to refuse a woman than he could refuse to breathe. Yet now, he felt only the expectation of enjoying a night of pleasure with Katla, not a life-threatening need to couple with as many women as possible.

Another change caused by her? Had she some power of her own, one given by the same source as his, that restored balance and control to his life? Gavin finally realized that he was hesitating to take a beautiful woman to his bed, and he laughed aloud.

"This is not something I do," he tried to explain.

"That is not what I have heard," she said.

He laughed again. "I meant bringing a woman here and not tearing her clothes off and having my way with her."

She did not smile politely in reply or look away; she trembled, her body shivering in arousal, not fear, and he felt desire course through him. This time though, it was desire the way he used to experience it before his power went awry. An increasing urge, not an out-of-control hunger. A pleasurable awareness of her body, not mind-emptying lust. A building desire to be with her, not an unavoidable one.

Like a man should feel.

But there were other needs pulling at him, and the strongest one was for sleep. Astonished, he realized that his body still craved that which had eluded him for so long. Undisturbed sleep. And with the comfort of his bed so close at hand, he found it difficult not to seek.

"Would you mind if . . . ?"

How could he ask her to sleep with him when she expected something else? Would she laugh at him?

"But for one or two nights, I have not slept soundly in months," he blurted out.

"Sleep then, if that is what you need," she answered.

For all his days, he would remember the look of disbelief on her face when he declared his need for sleep. Truly, he did not believe he'd said it either, but knowing that she would be there, in his bed, in his arms, removed the unnatural urgency that usually pulsed through him. As did the entire, sleepless night they'd spent together.

"Would you give me leave to unpack my things or should I join you now?"

He laughed again at her practicality and his own behavior. "Do as you wish. Consider this your home."

Gavin turned then, torn between watching her and getting into bed. He decided he could do both, so he undressed and climbed under the bedcovers. She moved quietly around the room, first folding his clothes and then her own. It was soothing in a way. She went from task to task, efficiently, silently, until her belongings were put neatly away.

Katla could feel his gaze follow her as she sorted through the clothing and possessions she'd brought with her, doing as he'd suggested and making this place her home. For the next month, it would be. The cave was not so bad as one might expect. The earl had provided every comfort possible and made this a place fit for his counselor to live. She ignored the growing heat within her and finished her task before facing him.

The Truthsayer was not what she'd expected at all. After the night they'd shared, she'd imagined carnal pleasures with little preamble or conversation at all. But now that seemed less important to him. When she'd expected another scandalous request or command, like his demand that she pleasure herself, instead he asked for sleep.

Haakon had placed something else on the table, something that Gavin had not mentioned—a small bottle filled with a dark-colored liquid. She'd seen this one before and knew it contained some healer's brew. Katla lifted it and held it up before the light of the lamp. He'd dosed himself with it several times while she observed from above

When he saw her looking at the bottle, he offered, "I do not sleep easily or enough."

"Your pardon," she whispered, bowing her head in apology. " 'Tis not my place to . . ." Every word she thought of sounded wrong.

"Snoop?" he finished.

She felt her cheeks burn.

"Aye," she admitted, placing the bottle back on the shelf. "My curiosity is unseemly." She wiped her sweaty, nervous palms against her tunic, drying them before facing him. "My father and his wife ever complained of it."

"You should know where that potion is," he said, nodding to it. "If I need it . . ." He did not finish, but she understood, having seen him consume it several times.

She changed the topic to something more mundane, away from all the questions she wished to ask. They had a month— there would be time enough.

"Should I put out the lamps?"

Though she done shocking things in his presence, she was not yet comfortable with bedplay, and did not wish to undress before him. Katla suspected that the scent his body gave off during arousal eased those inhibitions and allowed her to do many things with ease. Now, though . . .

"Leave the one by the doorway burning, but you can put the others out."

When she'd done so, she walked to the wooden chest in the corner and undressed quickly. Folding her tunic, gown, and linen shift, she placed the garments on top of the wooden trunk and then unlaced her shoes and stockings and removed them. Despite the heat given off by the brazier burning there, the chamber carried the chill of the rocks. She shivered as she turned toward the bed.

He lifted up the furs and blankets and held them for her to climb in. The lamp's light flickered as it touched his naked skin and his face. And though most of his body was covered by the bed linens, it was easy to see his aroused cock.

So much for going to sleep, she thought as she slipped into the large, very comfortable bed and into his muscular, heated embrace. So much for sleep.

Chapter Thirteen

When they approached the crest of the hill, Katla lost her breath. Not from the exertion of climbing up that hill, but from the sight before her. There, between this ridge and the farther one, sat a small, but perfectly circular group of standing stones. She took Gavin's outstretched hand and walked at his side down the hill toward the stones.

This day, her third with him, had been the first since their arrival to dawn with a clear sky. Haakon had packed food in a sack, and ale in a skin, before they set out. Gavin had kept their destination a secret, telling her only that there would be a surprise to see. It took hours to reach the stones, walking over gentle rolling hills, and even at this distance, they were spectacular.

"How did you find this place?" she asked. The circle was off the path that followed the coast between villages.

"Exploring when I was a boy," he said. "I grew up and lived near Durness my whole life. One summer my father told me of the stones and so I went looking for them when I could."

The descent grew steeper now as they made their way down into the valley toward the stones. The sun's rays flickered off them, sending shiny bits of light into Katla's eyes.

Soon, they reached the bottom and the ground leveled, making walking easier. Gavin held out the ale skin to her, and they paused for a moment.

"Have you visited the other stones?" he asked, wiping his mouth after taking a swallow of the ale. "On the mainland?"

"The ones near the ancient cairns?" she asked. "Aye."

Standing stones and ancient cairns were strewn across Orkney, the largest on the mainland where the earl lived. The Norse had visited them for centuries, especially Odin's Stone near the lake at Stenness, where oaths were sworn and promises made.

"These are different," he declared as he began to walk closer to the seven stones. "Come."

And they were, for as Gavin and Katla approached the ring, it was clear that each of the seven gray stones was actually cut or had been cleft by wind and rain into three sections. The surface of each glimmered in the sun, flecks of metal or some other kind of stone giving the appearance of silver and gold. Gavin did not walk into the circle—he walked around it, leading her three times along the perimeter before taking her near the ring.

"The rays of the setting sun on the summer solstice make this one appear afire, Katla. It is a sight to behold."

He reached out to lay his hand on the tallest of the stones, a simple gesture but one that was almost reverent. Gavin paused just before his hand came to rest on the stone, closing his eyes, as though listening for something.

"What do you hear?" she asked. Did his powers connect to something here?

He shook his head, laughing. "Nothing. Though as a boy, I thought I could hear laughter echoing through these stones. And sometimes, as I walked the circle, whispering seemed to follow me."

She smiled, thinking of how he must have been as a boy.

He placed his hand on the surface of the stone then and sighed. Katla reached out and placed her hand on the stone, too, to feel what he was feeling. He covered her hand with his, sealing it between the heat of his skin and the heat that emanated from the stone's surface.

"The legends speak of the Old Ones who lived among the stones eons ago, Gavin. Mayhap you heard the echoes of their lives?"

"Aye, you might have the right of it, Katla. Old Ones, Old Gods, ancient peoples—all may have lived here, arranging these stones. Mayhap they even performed pagan fertility ceremonies to ensure a good harvest or many children?"

Before she knew what he was about, he grabbed her hand and pulled her into the center of the circle, where the grass was level and thick. In the true center, a small area lay higher than the rest, and that was where he took her.

"I have heard stories that virgins were sacrificed here, at the very heart of the circle."

This lighthearted teasing was new. Each day, he seemed less burdened, less haunted, less madman. He drew her into pleasure with little or no provocation, and she discovered it was no hardship for her to join in his bedplay. Whether it was in his bed, along the river that ran through the cave, on the beach under the stars, or as it seemed likely, in the center of a ring of ancient stones. Katla smiled back at him.

"So do you mean to sacrifice a virgin or simply celebrate fertility here?" she asked, laughing at the surprise in his eyes. "I fear I can be of no help with one, but may be willing to participate in the other."

His eyes darkened, and her body reacted to that sign she was coming to know well. Soon, that scent, full of musk, and irresistible male attraction, would begin and she would be under his spell. Or not, for she could push it away and enjoy being with the man rather than the Truthsayer.

"I could play the virgin," he offered, peeling off his tunic and loosening his trews. He tossed his cloak on the ground and smiled. "A virgin must be taken before sacrifice. You could"—he paused and lowered his head, narrowing his gaze as she met it—"you could take me, Katla."

Though each time they joined was different from the rest, he'd never been able to lie still and allow her to explore his body as he'd explored every inch of hers. Heat shot through her as she considered all the places she could touch. Her own skin began to tingle as she imagined the touch and taste of his. Deciding to join his game, she nodded.

"I think I will," she whispered.

Giving him no chance to react, she kicked out her leg and took him down to the ground with a move she'd used dozens of times on Kali. Gavin landed with a thump, and she jumped on top of him, spreading her legs so that she straddled him. Instead of fighting back, he lay there and watched her with hooded eyes.

"Will you resist?" she asked, knowing that he was stronger and could reverse the situation if he chose to do so.

Gavin lifted his arms and tucked his hands behind his head. The movement made the muscles of his stomach and chest tighten and ripple. She could feel the strength of his thighs as he shifted beneath her weight. "Touch me," he said in a deep voice. "Take me, Katla."

Katla had never taken the first step in bedplay. Harald had been the first man for her, and their joinings were accomplished quickly, quietly, and usually in the dark. Gavin turned out to be exactly the opposite, for he seemed to enjoy teasing and tormenting her body until she was screaming for her release. He thought nothing of lying with her outside in the cool night air, or like this, in the light of day.

She did not think she'd ever found release when coupling with Harald, while Gavin would not spill his seed until she'd peaked several times and begged for him to finish with her. She suspected that Harald tried to be kind, for she thought he might feel some guilt that he'd taken her maidenhead. Gavin relished every joining, be it slow or fast, tender or forceful, and he always wanted more from her.

How would she return to the household of Harald Erlend-son after this interlude with Gavin? Katla decided she would savor every moment of it before life brought misery or heartache to her door.

Gavin recognized the moment Katla decided to accept control of their coupling, and he waited, holding his breath to see her first move. Her weight on his legs was not one that would hold him down, but he wanted to let her have her way with him this time. When she climbed off him, he wanted to protest, but waited instead to give her time.

He held his breath as she leaned down and kissed his mouth.

With a hand on the ground at either side of his head, she dipped down and kissed him again. Her unbound hair flowed around them like a curtain, shielding them from the outside and allowing him to take in her scent. She tested his lips with her tongue, and he opened to allow it in.

Bold strokes soon replaced her first tentative movements, and when he offered his tongue to her, she suckled on it. Gavin fought to keep his hands still, but his body screamed for him to move. He concentrated on her and on the almost musical sounds created in her blood and in her flesh as her body grew ready for him.

Katla lifted her mouth from his and began to kiss her way down his neck and then over his shoulders and chest. He arched against her when she touched one of his nipples and teased it with her teeth as he'd done to hers. He exhaled the breath he'd been holding and then sucked in deeply when she moved to the other one and bit him.

When she began to move down onto his stomach, his prick surged against the fabric of his trews. Gavin panted as she reached down and encircled his hardness with her hand. Between her tongue tracing down the muscles of his stomach and her fingers massaging the hard flesh in her hand, he struggled not to spill his seed. Her hair trailed over his skin, leaving it tingling in its wake. Then she paused, with her head so close to his prick he could feel her breath on it, and he let out a groan at the thought, at the wish, that she would take him in her mouth. Katla leaned back and met his gaze, a question in her eyes.

Gavin tried to imagine how it would feel when she took him in her mouth, but none of those guesses and no previous experiences prepared him for her. Her actions were uncertain, tentative, halting, as though she'd not done this before, but regardless of whatever inexperience she showed in the way she tasted him, his body bucked and thrust as soon as she drew him inside. He clenched his jaws tightly and tried not to frighten her.

"Am I doing that the wrong way?" she asked, her voice throaty and sensual as her body began to warm with her own arousal. "Should I stop?" Her gaze displayed genuine concern.

He barked out a rough laugh then. "If that is the wrong way, my angel, I may not survive it when you discover the right way."

She smiled at him as though he was being kind, but he was simply stating the truth—she would kill him with pleasure if she kept this up. And from the way she took him in even deeper then, using her tongue and teeth along his length and around the thick head of his prick, his survival would be a near thing.

Gavin leaned his head back, thinking that not watching her would make it easier to control his raging lust. He tried to ease the breaths in and out, listening to the lovely way her own breathing was growing rapid and shallow and trying to ignore the scent of her body as it blossomed with heat. Her heart raced and the flesh between her legs grew wet and ready—he could hear it all. He had nearly gained control when she lifted his balls into her hand and felt the sac with her fingertips, caressing it until it clenched in readiness. She teased the curls around his prick until he lost the control he'd fought so hard for and begged her.

"Angel! Too much . . . I beg you . . . cease . . . or I will . . ."

And he did. His body shook and trembled, and his release poured from him as did a long moan of pleasure as she sucked him dry and then licked her lips like a sated cat. But her body told him otherwise.

Gavin slid his hand under her gown and tunic and discovered just how aroused she was. Her body wept on his fingers and he used the moisture to ease his way as he plundered her for her own release. It took little time, for the folds there swelled and the tiny bud that could make her scream pulsed against the tip of his finger.

Katla rode his hand, sliding back and forth, trying to hasten her release. He pressed on, rubbing and caressing her until he heard her blood sing. Her body opened to him, arching, and he did not slow or cease.

He watched as her head dropped back and she screamed out as her body tightened and then released, the sound of her pleasure echoing around the stones and down the valley.

"Next time, I want you to ride my cock the way you rode my hand, Katla."

A new wave of throbbing answered him, then another release. Another moan escaped from her lips and he continued to massage that sensitive place between her legs. Determined to be inside her when she next came, he stroked softly and slowly, keeping her body aroused. When her eyes finally focused on his face, he smiled.

"Ride me, my angel. Ride me now."

Though she thought herself in control of this, it was clear that he truly was. With the pulsing waves of pleasure still making her ache and throb and *want*, she did not care. His reaction to her mouth on his cock was more than she'd expected and it made her body weep with desire. He eased his fingers in and out of her, soothing and exciting with the same stroke until she wanted more . . . again.

"Ride me," he repeated, and she wanted to obey. But how?

He motioned and she followed his guidance, standing first and tugging her tunic and gown and shift over her head, tossing them aside and then standing over him, her legs wide, exposing that heated place to his view. He reached up and she held her breath, waiting and waiting as he drew out the anticipation of his touch there. Katla arched against his hand once more while he stroked long and deep along her nether folds. Just as she would have screamed out another release, he stopped and placed his hands on her thighs, easing her down to her knees over his hips . . . and his cock.

Katla understood then and positioned her body so that he could guide his flesh deep into hers. And he did, filling her until she was seated completely on him. Then he urged her to move, placing his hands on her hips and lifting and sliding her until she found her own pace. Her flesh spasmed around his, clenching and holding and creating a friction that made her breathless. She moved slowly until the friction grew. Her quicker movements made him moan. Alternating the speed of her hips on his cock, she brought them both so close to release that it shocked her.

He touched her then, sliding his hand between her legs, urging her on, and bringing about her release with a flick of his finger there. Her inner muscles contracted against his flesh, but she did not stop until she felt the hot stream of his seed against her womb. Their cries of satisfaction mingled as his seed mixed with the wetness at her core, becoming one thing, one sound that traveled out and echoed off the stones standing sentinel to their act.

Exhaustion captured her quickly and she fell over, in his embrace, without moving off his body. He rubbed her back, smoothing her hair down over her like a covering. Katla knew not when his flesh left hers, but she did not have the strength to push herself off him. Just as her body urged her to sleep, the sounds began. She lifted her head, looking around for their source.

At first the sound resembled the tinkling of bells in the wind, but it changed and softened and echoed against the stones as the sounds of their releases had. Now, instead of bells, it was the sound of laughter floating in the air around them. The laughter faded, replaced by what she was certain were voices whispering. Katla looked again and found no one nearby.

Then, out of the corner of her eye she caught a faint movement near the shadows cast by the huge stones. But as quickly as she turned her head, it was gone. She thought she had imagined it, until she glanced at Gavin and realized he'd seen and heard something, too.

"Wee ones?" she asked, though they'd seen no signs that anyone lived within miles of this place.

"Nay, we are alone," Gavin answered, sitting up and helping her to sit next to him.

"But I heard . . . ," she began to explain. She stopped then, remembering his words about things he'd seen or heard here in the past. Maybe she'd just lost consciousness from too much pleasure and imagined it? "Mayhap those sacrificed virgins are whispering to us from the past?"

His face paled then, before he regained control and laughed at her suggestion. But she'd seen the expression in his eyes and knew he was hiding much from her. And mayhap what he hid from others was exactly what she needed to uncover to ensure that he would help Kali as he'd promised.

Chapter Fourteen

Gavin stood and collected their garments from where they lay strewn over the ground. He needed to avoid her astute gaze as she studied his reaction to her words . . .

And to the sounds they'd both heard.

Oh, he'd heard it before—the laughter, the whispering, even his name being spoken in the circle of stones—but never as clearly as he had this day. That no one but Katla had ever heard it was important in some way, but he did not know how. Did he dare to trust her with knowledge that no one else knew about him? Could she help him discover more than he'd been able to learn alone?

He retrieved the sack with their food and the ale skin from where he'd dropped them. When she finished dressing, she took the things from him and laid out their meal. Gavin still did not meet her eyes, busying himself with tying his trews back in place and putting on his tunic. Unable to avoid her any longer, he decided that he needed to try to trust someone.

"My parents found me here, in this very place," he said, accepting the piece of hard cheese she held out to him. Sitting down next to her, he watched as she took in what he'd said.

"You were a foundling?" she asked. "Here?"

"Aye. Before she died, my mother, the woman I called Mother, told me that on a late October night they were awakened by a stranger at their door. A young woman, my mother told me, one so pale she thought her ill, asking my parents to come here quickly. By the time my mother woke my father, the woman had disappeared."

"Was she your true mother then?"

Gavin took a swallow of the ale and shook his head. "I think not. My mother said she was too young to have borne a child. My father wanted to go back to sleep, but my mother urged him out of the croft and along the path until they got here."

"'Tis a wonder wild animals did not get to you first."

"That is not the strangest thing. My mother told me that all along the way, their path was brightened by strange lights that traveled along with them. Though it was the dead of night, they had no trouble finding their way here."

She paled then, as he had when his mother spoke of that night. "And you were here? In this spot?" She glanced around them at the small rise on which they sat.

"Aye. There was no one else here, so they took me to their home and raised me as their son."

They had been good parents teaching him his father's trade—farming—and never making him feel like the unwanted foundling he was. Even when the power that now controlled his life began to show itself, they never turned their backs on him. No matter what others thought or feared, he was their son and they loved him.

"When did they die?"

The question was not so startling, but the soft touch of her hand on his arm was. Katla seldom initiated any contact between them. He looked up from her hand to her face and found sympathy there.

"I had just left to live in Birsay when their croft burned to the ground," he answered, shivering as he remembered receiving the news. "No one could explain the fire or why they were unable to escape it."

He shrugged then, for he'd never understood how it had happened. But his life, there were many unanswered questions. He'd learned to ignore questions that could not be answered. And now, after reaching manhood, so many had been left unanswered.

"I need to learn not to pry into things that are not my concern," she said softly as her fingers caressed his arm. "I did not mean to bring up something so sad."

He shook his head. "I cannot come here without thinking of them, and since this was my idea, you are not to blame." He felt tears burning in his eyes and looked away, blinking against them. "Come. It will take a long time to get back to the cave," he said, standing and reaching out to help her up.

They followed the path out of the valley, back toward Durness on a different route from the way they'd come. He knew it would take them past his farm, his parents' farm, but Gavin found that he wanted her to see it. More than an hour passed before they approached it from the south.

Several men working in the field waved to him. He took Katla's hand and brought her to meet them. After his parents had died, Gavin wanted nothing to do with the farm, but Magnus suggested hiring someone to tend it. Gunnar and his wife and their sons were distant cousins of the earl and eager for the opportunity. And he'd proven to be a dependable man with a talent for coaxing crops from the fields, no matter the conditions or growing season.

Gavin watched Katla's reaction as the men approached and wondered at the sudden reluctance he could feel within her. When Gunnar invited them to stay for the evening meal, she stiffened next to him. Gavin said they would return on another day, and they left the farm behind. It was only when they approached Durness and she let go of his hand and allowed him to precede her through the village that he understood.

He had shamed her.

In such desperation that he cared for naught but his own needs, he'd ruined her honor by bringing her here. Harald had offered her an honorable place in his house, while Gavin offered her nothing but his bed. Worse, she had willingly accepted the humiliation to save her brother's life.

And Gavin knew not if he could even help her to do that.

He noticed the disapproval in the eyes of those they passed in Durness. Katla did not raise her head or say a word as he was greeted by villagers. She stood silently near him, behind him, never joining in the conversation, never moving closer and never being acknowledged by those around him.

He did not stop in the village often now and never brought a woman with him. He winced as he realized how he'd ignored the consequences his bed partners faced once they left him. The coins or gold he made certain Haakon gave them eased any guilt he may have felt and provided them with a dowry if they needed it.

Usually, there was no guilt.

If he was being honest with himself, he'd given little thought to those women after they fulfilled his needs.

Gavin glanced over at Katla then. They were about a mile out of the village and yet she still watched the ground as she walked. Any conversation between them had ceased at their encounter with Gunnar and his sons. As he observed her, noticing the flush in her face and the bleak expression in her eyes, he knew how much disrespect he'd brought on her.

Harald had warned him, but his relentless pain made him ignore the advice his friend had offered. He would have done nearly anything to possess Katla and to discover the source of her ability to mute the noise and to ease the pain in his mind.

Haakon had their evening meal prepared, and he left them

alone as soon as he'd served it. Katla ate little. Gavin watched as she pushed food around in the bowl before giving up and pushing it away. When he'd finished, she cleaned up the bowls and put out the lamps in the outer chambers. Gavin found her already beneath the bedcovers in his chamber when he arrived.

He undressed and climbed into the bed, expecting that she would resist any intimacies between them. So, when he touched her shoulder and she turned, moving into his arms, he was surprised. Their joining was quick and she seemed almost frantic when he brought her to her release and then sought his. As he drifted off to sleep, a disturbing realization floated into his thoughts. This coupling had been the first time that he had not heard her body's response and pleasure.

When he woke in the night and she was gone from his bed, terror struck him squarely in the heart. He pulled on his trews and went in search of her.

She could not sleep.

In spite of the miles walked and the physical exertion of coupling twice with Gavin, she'd lain awake until the deepest part of the night. Her mind and her heart raced with all the truths she'd learned this day. Wrapping a blanket around her and taking the lamp to guide her way, she'd slipped from the bed. She'd crept out of his chamber, walked through the outer cave, and crossed the wooden bridge that led to the beach. The tide was out, so the water had receded a distance from the mouth of the cave. Katla had found a dry place and sat on the sand, hugging her knees to her chest with the blanket around her shoulders.

Fool! she thought to herself as she reflected on the day's revelations about not only Gavin but also herself.

Somehow she'd convinced herself that all would be well at the end of this folly and that with her brother's life saved, she could go back to the life she'd led before her father's death. That had been her ultimate hope, and she'd pursued it fiercely, never seeing how her life would be changed by the course she followed.

Harald had tried to warn her, but Sven's daughter was known to be stubborn, and now she would pay the price for disregarding his wise advice.

Katla could blame her mistake on her inexperience, for she'd rarely left her home on Gairsay, and then only when accompanied by her father's wife or servants. Other than visits to the market or to attend the earl's feasts, her life had centered on her father's household, especially once his wife died.

But it was not truly inexperience that had caused her current predicament.

She could only blame her weak heart. Always, she'd longed for her father's approval. When he'd asked her to save his son's life, there was a gleam of pride in his gaze that spoke of his confidence she could do it. She'd wanted to so badly make him proud.

Katla had convinced herself that doing something wrong, if it was done for the right reasons, could be justified. That allowing the man who could save her brother to use her body was somehow as honorable as the purpose she pursued. But their encounters today had left her heart and soul battered and bruised.

Gunnar had looked away quickly enough, not allowing himself to stare at the woman Gavin had brought to his farm, but his sons, younger even than Kali, had not bothered to hide their open appraisal of her. They exchanged a look that told her they understood her place in Gavin's life.

Then, in the village, the people who had once greeted her as a stranger now treated her as less than dirt, looking away when she met their gaze, not speaking to her or acknowledging her. Once again, the younger men leered openly at her, not bothering to hide their heated glances and lewd gestures from her.

Both incidents had shaken her badly and made her understand what cruelty she would face if she was unsuccessful in saving Kali. She was a whore now, but his protection would allow her to seek a quiet life once he took over their father's lands. If he was executed, she would lose not only her brother but her only hope of a decent life.

Katla laid her head on her knees and closed her eyes, fighting off the tears that threatened to spill. She did not know how long she stayed like that, for she fell into a fitful sleep for short bits of time, but when she opened her eyes, Gavin stood nearby staring down at her.

Ah, she thought, he'd awakened and noticed she was not there. She needed to remember that she was there to give him pleasure, and she should always ask before leaving his bed. For this month, she must answer to him in all matters, but especially this one. Katla gathered the edges of the blanket but lost her balance as she tried to stand. Her legs, too long in one position, would not hold her, and she stumbled and would have fallen had Gavin not caught her and lifted her in his arms.

"Have a care," he whispered, holding her against his chest.

"I am fine. I can walk," she said. She waited for him to place her back on her feet, but he walked over the bridge and into the cave still carrying her.

"The floor is damp and slippery. I know it well," he said.

Katla would have to admit that being carried in his arms was no hardship at all, and it spared her bare feet from the rough ground. She settled in his arms, fearing that moving too much would throw his balance off as he made his way back to the bedchamber deep inside the rock. They made the short journey in silence, though she thought that she should ask his pardon for not being there when he wanted her. When he placed her feet on the floor, she faced him.

"I did not mean to anger you," she began.

"You did not, Katla." He shook his head. "I woke and found the bed empty. I worried that you might slip or fall."

So stunned was she by his admission, she could not remember what she wanted to say. "I did not mean to worry you," she whispered.

"Here, get under the bedcovers. You must be freezing from sitting on the beach with only a blanket to protect you."

Katla did as he told her and watched as he took off his trews and climbed in beside her. When her feet touched his leg, he shuddered.

"You are freezing!" he said, tucking the covers around her legs and gathering her close against him.

Within minutes, she was warm, very warm. But the cold made her ask, "Why have you chosen to live in this cave? I have seen your chambers in the earl's house. Why would you seek this place instead of the comforts there?"

She thought he might not answer, for the pause between her question and his reply was a long one.

"Mayhap I just like being alone, where others will not bother me," he replied, sounding as uncertain of the answer as she was.

Katla sat up against the headboard of the bed. "But you bring people with you, to you. Nay, that is not the reason." She searched his face for any sign that her manner of asking had offended him. Seeing none, she pushed again. "Something happened about eight months ago that caused you to seek out whatever this cave offers you."

"How do you know this?" he asked, his voice quiet and somehow more dangerous.

Sighing, she decided to be truthful with him. "I do not

think I am the only one who noticed this change, though I suspect no one in the service of the earl would dare to ask you about it," she explained. "When I began my search, I gathered what knowledge others would share—some of it spoken of boldly and some of it in hushed whispers." Katla watched as he listened. "Your power is feared. Your ritual is feared. You are feared, Gavin. So, though many notice, none will ask one so favored by the earl and one who possesses the power to read a man's thoughts."

"None save you."

She swallowed deeply, trying to decide whether he was angry or not. He lay on the bed, hands crossed behind his head as he'd laid earlier in the middle of the stone circle. But he did not meet her gaze. "I did warn you of my unseemly curiosity, did I not?"

Gavin laughed aloud, the sound of it filling the entire stone chamber. He did seem genuinely amused by her reply, but she also noticed he'd not answered her question. He rolled onto his side then, bracing his head up on one hand, and stared at her, almost daring her to ask him again.

So, she did.

"Tell me, Truthsayer, why do you live in a cave?"

Chapter Fifteen

Katla dared much, asking him what no one else would. But did he dare to tell her the true reasons for his move here? The force of his need to share his burden burned through his blood, nearly as strongly as the need for pleasure. It pushed everything else aside and surged forward. Gavin began to speak before he'd thought all the words out in his mind.

"The noise," he said, trying to think of how to explain the powers he had and the ways they were changing. She frowned at his words and shook her head. "I need the noise of the ocean and the river that feeds into it."

"But why, Gavin? It is enough to drive a person mad with the constant rushing. I have been here only a few days, and sometimes the loudness of the waves makes my head ache," she said. "I do not understand."

Gavin sat up and slid back next to her. "Over these last months, as the full moon approaches, the thoughts of others fill my head. The sounds, the voices, jumble into a chaotic clamor. It gets louder with each passing day until the ritual." He paused to see if she seemed to comprehend his words. "By the time the moon is dark, the pain becomes intolerable."

"The spirits? The healer's brew?" she asked.

"Aye. I tried both, but neither one blocks the sounds or the pain."

"Are these the thoughts of others around you or the thoughts of those you have heard during the rituals?"

He could not help the smile on his face. With but a few questions, she'd clarified some of his own thoughts. This was exactly what he had hoped for in daring to tell her the truth.

"I have believed them to be the thoughts of others around me, but you said something today that makes me think otherwise."

"I did? What did I say?"

"At the circle, you asked if mayhap I heard the echoes of those who lived there before. I have always thought the clamor in my head was made of the thoughts of those around me, for it worsens when I am near people. After thinking on your words, I begin to suspect the thoughts are those I have heard during the ritual."

He felt like the weight of all the rocks around him was lifted from him then. Admitting his weakness, speaking of it to another, had not made it worse.

"So you come here because there are so few people and to use the noise of the rushing water to drown out the sounds in your head?"

"Aye. Exactly."

Katla shook her head. "But you have said nothing about the pain, nothing about the thoughts you hear. Do you hear them now?" Her eyes brightened and she answered her own question. "Not since the night in your chambers. You were answering the voices in your head when you yelled aloud to leave you alone."

She pushed back the bedcovers and walked to the shelves on the other side of the chamber. Lifting the small bottle that held the healer's brew, she peered closely at it, tilting it to see its contents. "You have taken none of this, nor drunk strong spirits in days. Has the pain eased?"

This would be the most difficult thing to explain to her. She would laugh at him, think it simply a ploy to get her into his bed. Sweet Christ, he did not understand it himself! He watched as she walked back to the bed and sat there, waiting for him to speak. He reached out and took her hand in his, whether just to touch it or to hold her there when she heard his explanation, he knew not.

"When I had twenty-and-one years, the power struck me like a bolt of lightning in a storm. Though I'd had glimmers of it before that, every month as the moon reached its fullness, I could hear the thoughts of people around me. When I touched someone, I could hear their thoughts clearly. Each month the power grew stronger and stronger."

Katla nodded and climbed back under the covers next to him. "That was years ago?" she asked.

"I am nearing twenty-and-eight years now."

"An old man to be sure." She smiled.

"Aye," he said.

"Last year, just after the anniversary of my birth, it all began to change. The power grew stronger each month, but the noise in my head began, too. A low noise at first that I thought might be my imagination, it grew louder and louder until these last few months have become unbearable. Other needs have grown stronger at the same time. . . ." Gavin did not think he needed to explain which needs they were, and her blush made it clear she understood.

"Do you think it is leading to something? Escalating to some higher ability?"

Her questions were both insightful and intelligent. She saw patterns where he had not. She understood aspects he'd not considered. "'Twould seem to be, Katla. Though toward what, I know not. Mayhap my power will end then?"

"Or grow even stronger?" she asked. "You did not answer my question yet, Gavin, though if you do not wish to, I understand."

He laughed then. "Come, my determined Katla," he said, drawing her into his arms and sliding them both down on the bed. In spite of how upset she'd been, she did not hesitate. "I believe you are the reason the pain is gone."

Katla leaned back, trying to see whether he was jesting, but his intense gaze told her that he meant what he'd said. "How could I be the reason? Why would you think such a thing?"

"Last month, just as the moon turned from waning to waxing, I was visited by an angel. When the pain began to worsen, this angel appeared to me and had her way with me." She began to object that no such thing had happened, when he placed his finger on her lips to stop her.

"You see, as the pain grows, so too does my need for sexual relief. I seduced the angel to my bed, or the floor where I'd fallen, I think, and when my flesh joined with hers, a blessed silence replaced all the screaming in my head."

"Silence?" she asked. "When we coupled?" 'Twas difficult to believe such a thing. "And the pain?"

"Gone." He caressed her cheek and smoothed her hair away from her face in a touch so tender it nearly made her cry. "I cannot explain any of this, and I did not even believe you were real when I woke. Haakon had brought no one to me. There was no sign of you, but I slept for hours that night, undisturbed by voices or pain. You had disappeared, but the effects of whatever you did to me lingered, giving me the power to push away the clamor and the pain."

Of all the things she'd thought she might hear from him, this was the last she might have imagined. He thought she had some power to calm the painful noises that burdened him. That explained much to her—his demand for Harald to bring her to him when he'd recognized her at the ritual, the way he took her, possessing her body over and over again that first night, and his insistence that she accompany him here. He believed he needed her.

He watched her now, awaiting her reaction to his revelation. For once in her life she knew not what to say. Should she reassure him? Should she accept that she could give him the silence his mind needed? Why did joining their bodies cause such a thing to happen?

Katla could not discern the truth right now. She was overwhelmed by the events of the last several months. Grief, fear, and guilt all lay heavy on her heart, and she feared making another misstep. She needed to think on all he'd told her when she was clear headed and not lying next to the man asking her to believe him.

"And now?" she asked. "The dark of the moon approaches."

"Silence and no pain," he said, smiling. "I can push the noise away when it threatens. Since you entered my bed."

His bed. Not his heart or his home. His bed. Katla steeled her heart. It was clear to her that he hungered for relief from the pain, and the clamor in his head. If having her in his bed gave him relief, he would pursue her relentlessly.

"And you think this respite will continue until the ritual itself?"

"I know not. I only know that you have made a difference in my life."

She could think of nothing to say to him. Plagued with doubts and fear, Katla dared not reveal too much of her feelings to him now. When she did not reply, he smiled and nodded at her.

"I fear I have frightened you this night when I only meant to ease any fears or uncertainty you have. About today," he began, but she was the one to stop him with a finger on his lips.

"Nay. There is nothing to say about this day," she urged.

Her true feelings lay too close to the surface now. She did not want to expose any more of herself to him. She only had to make it through two more weeks and then they could return to Orkney and save her brother. For just a little longer, she needed to shield her heart. "I was feeling maudlin tonight." She held her breath as he studied her face. He nodded and guided her into his arms. His warmth soothed her. She felt herself drifting toward sleep and then she remembered the question that had begun these revelations. She smiled as she realized he'd not answered it fully.

"So, why do you live in this cave . . . now?" Katla asked. But she fell into sleep's clutches before she heard any answer he might have given.

Chapter Sixteen

Gavin heard the sleep-slurred words whispered as she fell asleep and he wondered. Why did he continue to live here in the cave when her presence seemed to give him the control he needed? Two days later when a storm struck, stranding them within the interior chambers and assaulting them with slashing rains and howling wind, Gavin decided he'd had enough of the cold and damp place that had been his haven.

With a few orders to Haakon and with the help of some of the men from the village, his furnishings and belongings were moved from the cave up to the small croft above it. Haakon seemed happy to stay in the village, and Gavin suspected that a young widow named Helga had something to do with his willingness to make the move.

In a way, he felt that the change from the darkness of the cave to the light of the cliffs above was like being born again. Without the constant anguish, he could live as a normal man would, and with Katla at his side, he felt like one. For the first time in so long, he even traveled back to his farm and worked a day with Gunnar and his sons. Walking the furrowed earth, digging hard and long, satisfied something within him that he did not realize had been unfulfilled.

Though Katla seemed withdrawn and quiet at times, he reminded himself that her life was in turmoil, her father recently dead, her brother facing execution. Gavin tended to forget that she was young as well. She'd always lived in her father's household, protected by his name and his presence until just months before, and now she faced an uncertain future.

Despite a desire on his part to help her, his own future was not clear. He realized he wanted more from her, wanted a life together, but he believed he would not survive for more than a few rituals. Any hope for the future lay quietly inside him, awaiting the upcoming ritual to determine whether Katla had made a difference after all.

But each night holding her, he allowed himself to imagine a life with her, the kind of life his parents had lived—working side by side, living, celebrating, loving, mourning—whatever life and the fates threw at them. This time together seemed idyllic, even when he began to feel the power building and surging within him as the full moon approached.

The day came for them to return to Orkney, and he noticed the change in her immediately. Any hint of playfulness or whimsy she'd shown over the past weeks lay hidden now. Though he asked her to talk about her fears, she just gazed through haunted eyes and remained silent.

The only thing that was a constant for them was the pleasure they shared. She'd never turned from him or withheld herself after that one time, and the sound of her body as he aroused her and brought her to release was nearly as pleasurable as the act itself. His need for her did not lessen, but it was tempered, easing from frantic craving to simple desire.

Haakon packed what they would need, and Gavin hoped

that he could convince her to return to the croft with him, to stay with him, after the ritual. But he waited, knowing that there were too many variables ahead of both of them. Worse, Gavin was not certain he could save her brother's life. He might condemn her brother and not even know it. In the entire time they'd been in Durness, she'd never confided in him about what was to come. When she spoke of her brother, it was about his innocence or his sense of humor and their enjoyment of playing pranks on others. But as he stood watching the approach of the boat that would carry them north, she touched his back.

"Gavin," she said quietly before he turned to face her. "You will help him, will you not?" She leaned her head against his back. He could feel her words against his skin as she spoke. "I beg you. . . ."

He'd seen little vulnerability in her during these weeks together, other than that night he'd shared so much about himself with her. The way her voice trembled and the way she grasped his tunic spoke volumes about her fears. His heart pained him, because he was unable to promise much to her. The earl usually determined who would be part of the ritual— it was their arrangement. Even while traveling elsewhere, Magnus would send word to Brusi the Lawspeaker, who oversaw the truthspeaking.

"I have never asked to hear the truth of someone before, Katla. The earl makes his choice and . . ."

"You must, Gavin! You promised that you would help him."

He turned then and met her tearful gaze.

"You told me you would grant anything I asked if I would come here with you." She twisted her hands and stared at him. "I fulfilled my part of the bargain. Now you must do yours."

"A bargain? This was only a bargain to you?" he asked. Gavin could not explain why her matter-of-fact words bothered him so much, but they did.

She nodded then, destroying any hope in his heart that something was growing between them. "I did this for my brother. No other reason."

He'd fooled himself into believing that her complete submission to him had been prompted by her feelings for him. She did not care that his end was nearing. She did not care that she had made a difference. She cared only for a boy who most likely would speak his truth and be damned for it. He wanted to hate her, but he could not.

"I will keep my part of our bargain, Katla. I will hear your brother's truth in Birsay. The boat is here. Get your things and meet me at the beach."

He left without another word to her.

She shielded her eyes against the sun and watched him leave the cottage. His anger poured off him so strongly, she could feel it. Anger and something else she could not identify. Katla wanted to call out to him and beg his forgiveness for what she'd said and how she'd said it. Instead she did as he told her to do and gathered her things together.

Katla glanced around the small cottage that had been like a home to her for these last weeks. Nothing remained of her here. Nothing to remind him of the time they'd shared. Nothing.

In three days, the full moon would give him power to hear the truth. He would hear her brother's truth, and Kali would be freed. Her life would be given back to her. Unfortunately, she'd given away a part of her heart that she suspected would never be hers again.

Packing the last of her gowns in the leather sack, she considered how things could be different for her and for Gavin. Not once during these weeks had he mentioned anything about what would happen between them after the full moon. Although he was content to play at living together in this cottage, he did not offer her a place here with him.

'Twas as Harald had warned, he would break her heart. From the pain that pulsed in her chest at the thought of never seeing Gavin again, she thought he might have indeed. Despite his kind treatment of her, his concerns for her comfort, and his changed behavior since they'd arrived here, he wanted no more from her than he had originally bargained for.

He wanted her for only the comfort he gained. He had never hidden his purpose from her and never pretended that his desire was anything else. Tugging her cloak on, she lifted her sack and closed the door behind her.

"He gets very tense as the full moon approaches," Haakon said quietly, taking the sack from her. "Sometimes he does not even notice it himself."

The man had spoken not a dozen times during her time here, so his words surprised her. That he seemed to seek to offer her comfort was still more surprising. "Is he the same as before?" she asked.

"Gavin said you witnessed him here before the last ritual. Is he different now?"

"Aye," she admitted. Anyone seeing him could tell.

"Come, the boat is ready," he announced, holding out his arm to her to help her down the steep slope. They'd almost reached the bottom when he spoke again, in a hushed tone. "You have showed him what it is to be only a man, not the Truthsayer. He will remember it."

Startled, Katla stopped, but Gavin called out to her then and she walked to him. Though he looked ready to say something to her, he did not. Soon they were all aboard the boat and prepared to sail north once more to Orkney.

Gavin seemed ill-at-ease as he paced along the railing of the boat. The day was calm and clear and they had good winds that moved them swiftly over the water. Once they passed Hoy and the port of Stromness, it would take only a few hours to reach Birsay.

She'd spent so much time alone with Gavin that she did not know how to be with him when others were near. Aside from a few short conversations and some shared glances, they remained at opposite ends of the boat during the voyage. As they arrived at the dock, she wondered, what was her place?

Should she walk at his side through Birsay to the earl's house? Should she stay behind and wait to be called? Should she hide her face and wear the shame that would be hers once she was recognized as Sven the Traitor's daughter and the Truthsayer's whore? Oh, God in heaven, she needed to speak to Kali before he learned of her disgrace!

"Come, walk with me," Gavin said as he climbed from the ship and held his hand out to her. She took it and soon stood next to him on the dock.

"I would see Kali if it is permitted," she said, knowing that she was Gavin's until the full moon passed.

"Harald is the one who can permit it or not, Katla. Haakon," he called out, "send word to Harald Erlendson that we have arrived. I would see him in my chambers."

"My thanks," she whispered as Haakon ran off to do Gavin's bidding.

Her hands shook now at the thought of walking through the center of the village to the earl's house. When Gavin began walking, she followed with her head lowered, meeting no one's gaze. They'd gone only a short distance from the dock when he slowed down and took her hand in his, squeezing it as he led her down the street.

As they reached the earl's house, Haakon caught up with them. He drew Gavin aside and whispered to him, not sharing his news with her. But a few sidelong glances at her during the hushed conversation told Katla it involved her. From the frowns and the furious exchange of words, it was not favorable news.

"Harald is not here in Birsay," Gavin told her when Haakon ran off once more. "We will talk in my chambers."

His arrival sparked a flurry of activity among those who lived and served the earl. Servants ran before them, carrying their clothing into Gavin's chambers. Trays of food appeared before them. Jugs of wine and ale, too. And women gathered in the corridor outside his chambers.

If she did not know of him and his reputation and needs, she would think him only an honored guest. But these women had come hoping to be summoned to his bed.

Katla could not explain the way her own body reacted. A wave of jealousy pierced her at the thought of his doing what they'd done together with someone else. Shaking it off, she knew that another, or others, would soon share his bed. It was a fact she knew well, even if her heart and soul did not want to believe it. Gavin noticed where her gaze fell and ordered the women all away.

Once the room was settled and all the servants dismissed, Gavin poured a cup of wine for her and waited for her to drink some of it before he began.

"A message was received two days ago from the Scots king about your brother."

"Kali? What did the king want with my brother?" she asked, dreading the answer. She sank onto a chair and drank down the rest of the wine.

"Word reached Edgar of the plot hatched by your father, and that your brother might have had knowledge of it. King Magnus ordered Kali turned over to the Scots king."

"Turned over? Where, Gavin? Where is Kali now?"

"The earl ordered Harald to take him to the Scots king in his main city in the east. They departed two days ago, in a vessel sent by Edgar. Harald left word that he will try to keep him alive."

"Try?" she asked, crying out in terror. "But Kali knows not of any plot. He cannot tell the Scots king anything!" she protested, running to him and grabbing his arm. "Gavin, we must go!"

The room began to sway around her. Katla reached out to steady herself, but the chamber grew dark as though a cloud moved in front of the sun. She watched Gavin reach for her, moving so slowly that she could see the muscles tense in his arms. The buzzing in her ears grew louder and louder until she screamed against the pain. Just as she realized that this must be what Gavin felt, everything turned black.

Gavin cursed his stupidity and grabbed for her just as she sank into oblivion. He lifted her in his arms and carried her into his bedchamber, laying her there until she could recover from this faint. He sought the washbasin, poured some water in it, and grabbed a cloth. Taking the cup of wine and sitting at her side, he dipped the cloth in the water and then dabbed her skin, trying to awaken her.

This had turned into a disaster.

From their angry departure from Durness, to the silence between them on the journey and now this, nothing had gone as Gavin wished it had. Part of him wanted to stay in Durness, alone with her as he had been these last weeks, living a lie even though he knew that the world around them would demand the truth soon enough.

He dipped the cloth again and wiped her forehead. She was sweating now, and her breathing changed as she awoke. Her gaze darted quickly around the room, from him to the door and back, as she tried to focus. Gavin lifted the cup to her lips and urged her to sip. After she took in a small amount, he put the cup down and let her get her bearings.

She was still wrapped in the long cloak she'd worn on the boat, so he unpinned the brooch holding it closed and loosened it around her neck.

"Better?" he asked softly. Katla nodded and tried to sit up. "Nay, do not. Give yourself a few moments to feel stronger."

He knew she wanted to be out of that bed, to do something to help her brother. He knew the first thing she would do would be to demand that he go to Dunfermline, the main city of the Scots king.

She had no idea of the impossibility of such a demand, but she would make it regardless. And he would have to refuse. Shielding himself from the thoughts of only these few hundred people in the vicinity of Birsay was a struggle. No matter her presence or the strength that her passion seemed to give him in controlling the pain and the clamor, he would not survive a journey to that city with its hundreds and possibly thousands of inhabitants.

His mind would shatter from the pain, and surely madness would follow. She was watching him closely now, and he waited for her to begin her assault.

Last month, the man he had been would have been able to refuse without guilt, without hesitation. But the man he was now had held her and loved her for a month and could not bear the thought of disappointing her or allowing her brother to die. He just did not have the strength to say aye.

He wanted to, he desperately wanted to be the man who could help her. He wanted to be the man who could love her and keep her. He wanted to be the man who lived to see her day after day. Unfortunately, the fates had something else planned for him, and he had no future to offer her.

Katla pushed herself up to sit, and he waited for the inevitable war to begin.

Chapter Seventeen

She pounded on the door and screamed until she had no voice left. Katla's hands were bloodied when she gave up, sinking to the floor in exhaustion. He'd had her locked in here more than a day ago, just as the full moon began, and he'd not been back since. Servants came. Servants with strong warriors accompanying them brought her food and forced her back into the small room once it was delivered.

Fighting them had been a mistake. Her face swelled where one had struck her when she'd tried to push her way out of the room. Askell was his name, and he apologized after it happened, but Katla had been more surprised than hurt by it then. Now, as she touched her cheek with the back of her hand, it hurt.

Three days wasted. Three days of a journey she should be making were already lost. And from the silence that answered her calls for release, more would be lost before they freed her from this prison. She crawled over to the corner away from the door and slumped against the wall. Pressing her hands against her gown to stop the bleeding, Katla tried to calm herself so she could come up with a plan.

The ritual had passed, and by now, Gavin would need pleasure to help him control the voices in his head. Would he call for her or another? If he believed that she offered something different, that he gained peace and control with her and no other, then he would summon her. If that was a lie, he would send out that scent and draw any number of women to him to ease his needs.

That possibility tormented her as much as knowing her brother could die at any moment.

And so she waited. Katla slept fitfully through the next several hours, drifting in and out of terrible dreams about both Kali and Gavin. She did not even realize she was awake when the door opened and Haakon entered. She would have jumped to her feet, but she had no strength left to fight him or the bulky warrior at his back.

Haakon stepped aside, and two women entered. He turned his back while they saw to her needs and cleaned and bound her hands. The women rubbed unguent on her swollen cheek, and they brought fresh clothing for her. Once their tasks were completed, they left as quietly as they came. All but Haakon, who crouched before her and spoke.

"He will free you when he can, Katla," he said.

"When will that be?" she asked hoarsely, accepting the cup he offered and drinking down the cold water. "Why is he doing this, Haakon? Why will he not go with me to the Scots king to save my brother's life?"

"Mayhap he cannot." Haakon stared at her as he spoke. "Mayhap he has reasons for refusing."

"A man's life is at stake. . . ."

"Aye, Katla, a man's life is at stake."

She was tired and she hurt and she just wanted to leave and get to her brother. She had not the time nor the strength for a battle of words with Gavin's servant. "Enough, Haakon. If you have only come to torment me, I beg you to go now and leave me in peace."

"I know he shared with you some of the details about how the voices and pain build before the ritual. Do you wish to learn the rest of it? To understand the man who lives through it?" Haakon stood and held out his hand to her. "To learn why he did this to you?" He glanced around the room and then back at her.

Katla stood, a little unsteady on her feet at first, but able to walk. She nodded when she was ready, and he led her out of the room and through the back corridor of the house to the part where Gavin stayed. Haakon took her through the chamber where the ritual occurred and then to the door of Gavin's bedchamber. Haakon turned and faced her, blocking the door with his body until he was ready to allow her inside.

"The power that surges through him does not simply end," he explained. "It burns him within until he cannot bear more, and then it leaves him empty."

Katla held her breath as he opened the door a crack for her to look. Gavin lay on the floor in the middle of the chamber, unmoving, unconscious. "You leave him there? On the floor?"

"It is safer for him."

As he finished the words, Gavin's body contorted and shook on the floor, writhing in pain. He clutched his ears and moaned. When he rolled over to his side, she caught a glimpse of his head, his ears. From within, they burned brighter than the brightest torch she'd ever seen! Haakon watched but did nothing to help his master.

"Haakon! Help him!" she cried.

"He had hoped that being with you would ease this as well," he said. "But it is unchanged since the last time."

Katla choked as she asked, "He suffers this every month?"

"With every ritual. Worse each time. Lasting longer each

time. Draining him more each time," Haakon explained. "As his powers to hear the truth grow, the punishment he suffers afterward grows, too." He pulled the door shut.

She shook her head. "How does such a flame burn within him and not kill him?"

"He knows not, only that it does. He's searched for answers for years and found no one who can help him understand this power, this gift, and the curse that seems to go with it."

"Why are you telling me this?" she asked. "If he wanted me to know, he would have told me."

"He told you more than he has revealed to anyone else, Katla. That means something," Haakon said quietly.

"But he kept this from me," she pointed out. "And he pushed me away, reminding me that only our bargain lies between us. He wants nothing more from me than that."

Haakon smiled then, and it took a few moments to realize that the smile did not reach his eyes. Sighing, she shrugged.

"I am exhausted and heartsick and can do nothing for him or for my brother. Since you showed me this, I beg you to tell me why."

"He will survive this, for it seems to be pain enough to torment and torture but not to kill him. When he does, you must offer him another bargain."

"Why would he accept it?"

"Because he needs you."

She shook her head and leaned against the wall. Katla ached and needed to sleep. She'd had no rest since they'd arrived here and discovered her brother gone.

"He said he could not go to Dunfermline. He would not explain. He would not discuss it, Haakon. He only proclaimed the impossibility of it and refused to explain himself. Why would he react so?"

"Fear," Haakon said. "He cannot explain what he does not

understand." Haakon crossed his arms over his chest and glared at her. "But I know that Katla Svensdottir fears nothing and would do what must be done. When he recovers, offer him a bargain that gives him a reason to conquer his fear."

Katla tried to think on his words, to make sense of the confusion in her mind, but she could not. "I will speak to him when he awakes. How long will that be?"

"This part lasts about three to four days," he explained.

"Three more days? I cannot wait that long before setting out after my brother and Harald. Gavin must know that. . . ."

"I did not say you would be able to speak to him in three or four days," Haakon began.

"Ah, good! Send word to me when I can speak to him," Katla offered.

"The next part could last over a week," Haakon said, putting up his hand to stop her from arguing with him. "You could speak to him sooner, but he will not hear you."

"You are confusing me, Haakon," she said, rubbing her forehead and wincing against the growing pain there. "Should I try to bargain with him or not?"

"The result of the burning you saw is that he will be deaf for some days after this and will not be able to hear any bargain you offer."

Her mouth dropped open in surprise. She'd never considered this, never realized the ritual had this aftereffect. "But I spoke with him last month, when he called me to him. I asked him to help my brother and he agreed. . . ."

"To whatever you asked him to do. He could not hear you, Katla. But whatever had happened between you gave him the belief, the hope, that you could help him. He was desperate for you and set me to search for you on our return to Durness. When you appeared before him and he realized you were real and no dream, he would have granted any request you asked of him."

He had promised her what she wanted and she'd never asked any questions. So desperate was she that Katla had accepted the word of a man she truly had no reason to trust. But she had now to discover that he'd blindly or deafly agreed—and would have done so to anything she'd asked.

Some idea, some thought, teased her mind but she could not grasp it now. After she'd slept and considered all this new knowledge Haakon had shared, she could come up with a plan to get to her brother. Katla straightened up from the wall and turned away from Haakon only to realize that she had no place to sleep now. Gavin lay senseless and in pain in his chambers and Harald was gone, so she hesitated to use his room. Haakon motioned to her to follow him, so she did.

The room he led her to in no way resembled the one where she'd been imprisoned for three days, but it was the same one. A bed, a chair, and her trunk now lay there, awaiting her arrival. She sank on the bed, needing rest more than she needed to undress. She was nearly in sleep's grasp when Haakon spoke once more as he pulled the door closed.

"Make him a bargain, Katla. Offer him what no one else can."

As she drifted to sleep, the question plaqued her. What could she offer that no one else had? He had all the women he could ever desire. He had unimaginable wealth as the gift of those priceless armbands and neck ring showed. He had every possible comfort. What could Katla offer him that was different? What did he need?

A possibility came to mind as sleep claimed her. She would need help and gold to see it happen—but she had one and could acquire the other. Within two days, she had her plans in place. Since he would not be able to hear her request for more

days than she could wait, she decided to take the decision out
of his hands.

For Katla had some good arguments to sway him in the
right direction.

Gavin waited until he could stay out of his bed for the entire day before he dared see her. She would be furious at him
for his refusal to chase Harald and Kali to Scotland and for
having her held so that she could not leave, either. He'd done
it for her safety—without his or Harald's protection, she was a
target for too many others who would like to see her go the
way her father had. Until he was recovered enough to protect
her, he'd ordered Haakon to keep her somewhere safe.

And with his usual zeal for competence, Haakon had.
Which was certain to have enraged her. Gavin did not look forward to facing an enraged, determined Katla Svensdottir. But,
he wanted to see her even if he could not hear her.

Walking toward the chamber where Haakon had held her,
he thought on what to say to her. He'd never revealed his
deafness to her. She did not know that he had agreed to what
she'd requested without hearing a word of it. She did not know
he believed that the ritual could lead directly and swiftly to
her brother's guilt and execution. She did not know that he
would have promised her anything, whether possible or not,
so that she would agree to return to Durness with him.

As he turned the corner, he decided that he must be honest
with her. If she understood his reasons, the risks he would face
confronting the thousands of inhabitants and their thoughts,
she would comprehend why he could not go after her brother.
If she knew how much she'd come to mean to him and how it
hurt to refuse her, mayhap she would. . . .

He reached the last corridor and saw her leaving, walking
away without seeing him. Haakon had said she was not locked

in any longer, but with her cloak on her shoulders and her bag in hand, she seemed to be going somewhere. Without time to summon Haakon, Gavin followed her down the corridor and out into the yard.

Leaving his chambers while deaf was not something he did, so the strangeness of being outside and not able to hear anything—not birdsong, not people calling out, not animals in their biers, nothing—struck him immediately. He stopped and turned around in a circle trying to hear a sound, but he saw everything moving by him in complete and utter silence. Gavin almost lost sight of Katla, so he hurried to catch up to her.

He remained some distance behind her, watching where she headed and what she did. Katla walked down the main street and then ducked into one of the smaller side alleys. He was not familiar with this section of the village, but he did not hesitate. Just as he made the next turn, he realized he was not in an alley, but in an enclosed area between two houses. Without being able to hear anything, Gavin could not listen for her footsteps. It took him only a few moments to know that he'd walked into a trap of some kind. He turned to escape, but someone hit him from behind and he fell into a black unconsciousness.

He stirred a few times while being moved, but with a hood tied over his head and his hands and feet bound tightly Gavin could not tell where they were taking him. The rag stuffed in his mouth kept him from calling out for help. The heat grew stifling, and he realized he was wrapped in a rug or tarp. As they placed him in a cart and it began to move, Gavin tried to figure out where he was being taken. Unable to hear or see, he accepted that he would have to wait and find out who'd planned this and why. His head spun as the cart or wagon hit another rut in the road, and he moaned against this new pain.

He could not tell how much time or distance had passed

when they came to a stop, and several pairs of strong arms lifted him from the wagon and carried him away. Then he could feel motion beneath them and knew he was on a boat or ship. Carried down steps, he thought, and then dropped on a wooden floor or deck. He ached from being tied up, from being hit over the head, and now from being dumped on the hard floor.

Hours later someone came, unrolled him from the heavy covering, and untied his hands from behind him. Before he could try to get the hood off to see who was responsible for this abduction, it was tied snugly around his eyes, and a jug was pushed into his hands. He was so thirsty, he drank it down without pause. When he finished drinking, a crust of bread was pushed into his hands. He understood the message—eat quickly. No sooner had he put the last bit in his mouth then a gag covered his mouth and his hands were tied once more.

Gavin could not hear a sound, but the feel of the ship's movements told him they were moving on the water. His arms grew numb as he struggled in vain against the ropes.

Deciding to conserve his strength for a chance to make his escape, he rolled to his stomach and rested his pounding head against the deck. He was inside a boat, a ship, big enough to have a covered deck or a lower interior deck. Whoever had planned this had wealth to pay for the use of such a vessel. Whoever planned this wanted him alive, for it would have been easier to kill him in that alley rather than to take him, unobserved, out of the village to a dock large enough for this ship. And there was no need to feed a man intended for death.

Whoever planned this had known he would follow Katla.

Would Godrod, her servant, have been so bold? Gavin knew of no one else who would act on her behalf. Did her brother yet have supporters who would do something like this? And to what purpose? He had never tried to force the power within him, but could he? Could it be used when demanded? He thought not, though he'd felt more in control of it during this cycle. Too many questions and no answers.

So he would wait. His hearing would return, soon he hoped, and then he would be able to discover who his abductors were. He had doubts, but he feared he know who was behind this scheme.

Her name was Katla Svensdottir.

Chapter Eighteen

Though his hearing remained clouded, his sense of smell worked only too well. And after what he thought had been four days at sea, the smell of his own skin was rank.

At first, he thought he must be far out at sea for there were few thoughts or sounds invading his mind. Then he understood that the control given by his joining with Katla was strong even now. With each passing day, though, the voices grew stronger and louder and it took more effort on his part to gather them behind the wall in his mind. He tried to keep them contained in that way as he had before, but that ability waned as the time since he and Katla had last made love increased. Gavin noticed, for he had plenty of time to consider such things, that he was not feeling the usual overwhelming sexual need. He laughed then, harshly, through a throat unused in days. For so many months he'd lived for the next nameless, faceless woman he would have and now when he could think of only one, she might be the person behind this.

As he feared, without Katla's physical presence, the clamor began to increase just as his hearing began to return. If he had more time and Katla with him, he might be able to determine if she really did make a difference. Their few weeks together were not enough to answer the questions raised about why she was different from every other woman he'd bedded.

When the ship slowed, Gavin prepared to learn his fate and the reason behind his taking. The vessel came to a stop, but it seemed as if hours passed before he felt footsteps on the floor of the chamber. Then without warning, they untied his feet and half dragged, half lifted him up to the main deck, where he was handed over the side. Now in a smaller boat, he felt others surrounding him and decided escape was not yet possible. They slid to a stop and once more handed him over the side and then walked him through shallow, cold water to the shore.

"Who are you? Where are you taking me?" His gag had been removed. He asked even though he was uncertain whether he would hear the answer given. "The earl will pay any ransom you ask for my return," he offered. Men desperate enough to do something like this might be willing to accept gold for his return. He did not know whether anyone responded to his questions.

Too many days of inactivity immediately after being drained by the ritual weakened him, and Gavin could hardly resist anything they wanted to do. He was pulled along, away from the shore and onto more uneven terrain, where he was helped over rocks and up a hill. Soon they drew to a halt, and he waited to meet his fate.

Instead, they removed the bindings around his wrists and loosened the rag tied around his eyes and pushed him inside a small cottage. As his eyes adjusted to the light, the door closed behind him and he heard a bar dropped into place. Turning around to look at this new prison, Gavin found it to be a strange one—for a large tub sat off in one corner of the main chamber. And it was filled with water!

He almost laughed as he noticed the bowl of soap, drying cloths next to the tub, and the clean set of clothing lying on the bed. The bed? Aye, a pallet covered in clean linens lay in the other corner, separated from the tub by a table on which a meal sat waiting for him.

Gavin knew there was much more to this, but the thought of being clean after so many days in the hold of a ship and the aroma of a hot, cooked meal convinced him to see to his needs first. He attacked the food, tearing apart the roasted fowl with his hands, peeling the meat from the bones and shoving it in his mouth. He found fresh bread and a crock of butter and another of soft cheese, and made quick work of the meal after days of shipboard food.

Finished with filling his belly, he decided to take advantage of the bath prepared for him. Why not? If whoever controlled this endeavor wanted him clean and comfortable, why should he refuse? Convinced his life was not in danger, he peeled off his dirty tunic and trousers and tossed them near the door. He unlaced his shoes and rolled down his stockings and left them near the pallet.

Gavin dipped his hand in the water—it was neither the warmest nor coldest bath he'd climbed into. He could not stretch his legs out, for it was a round tub and not oval shaped like the one in his chambers. Still, it was a pleasure to sink into the water and he reached over the side for the bowl of soap. Intent on the task, the gentle touch of a hand on his back surprised him. He dropped the soap and turned to meet Katla's equally surprised gaze.

Katla had to force herself away from Gavin on the ship. She'd watched from a hidden corner of the alley as he was taken by the men Godrod had hired. Selling off one of the gold arm-bands had provided her with enough coins to hire the ship and the men to sail it south to Scotland. And to kidnap the earl's truthsayer and bring him along on the voyage so that he could save her brother's life.

Though the need to keep him alive and well had been im-pressed on those hired, Godrod would not let her intervene in his treatment on the ship. Doubts had filled her as she'd watched Gavin tied and blindfolded below deck. She'd even called out his name once, but he was still deafened and did not hear her. It could be days more before he regained his hearing, but at least they would be miles and miles along on the journey to the abbey and palace at Dunfermline. When his gag had been removed and he'd begun calling out for help, she'd clenched her fists and fought not to go to him.

Once ashore, she'd given him some time alone before en-tering the cottage. Katla wanted to touch him, to ease his fears and to explain what she'd done but she waited. Words filled her mind, every possible thing to say, every argument to use to convince him to help her, but nothing seemed quite right.

Haakon had told her to offer him a bargain no one else could, and she thought she knew what that was—another month with her. It would be an easy thing for her to give. After spending weeks with him, fulfilling his every sexual need and experiencing pleasures she'd never felt before, she under-stood the bargain better than the last time she'd agreed to such a thing. The only difficult part would be keeping her heart untouched by him.

The twinge she felt as she watched him in the tub, un-kempt and deaf, told her it might be too late for that.

Now, though, she would need to persuade him to do some-thing he'd refused to do. The tightness in the pit of her stom-ach warned her of the danger in the course she'd chosen, but her need to save her younger brother, and to fulfill her promise to her father, pushed her forward. When he reached over and picked up the soap next to the tub, she touched his back to tell him she was there.

"Ah, you show yourself at last," he said, shifting away from her hand. He turned back and scooped some soap out, rubbing it over his skin and lathering it. "I wondered when you would step out of the shadows."

She said his name but he did not react—whether from inability to hear or his own stubbornness, she knew not. Reaching over, she snapped her finger and thumb behind his ear, where he could not see her action. Nothing. He was still deaf, so any explanations would have to wait. But it was clear he understood she was behind this kidnapping.

Did he hate her now? Taking him prisoner when he was most vulnerable and then keeping him tied up without explanation? Trying to force him to do something he'd refused to do? He might still refuse to perform the ritual with Kali. From his comments, she thought he had little control over his truthspeaking.

Could he stop it? Could he choose a different subject? She shuddered, thinking that all her efforts might fail and he would hate her for nothing.

He'd cleaned his chest and stomach and moved onto his shoulders. Katla noticed the scrapes on his back, probably from when they'd dropped him on the deck and when they'd dragged him along the alley. Guilt pierced her. Before she thought on it, she stepped closer and dipped her hand into the soap. Kneeling behind him, she spread it on his back, dabbing it gently on the injured places. He stiffened beneath her touch and then relaxed as she rubbing the soap into a lather and used both hands to clean his skin.

The feel of his muscles under her hands reminded her of

many, many other times when one touch led to another and another, and heat spread through her. Would he accept her body now that she'd done this? Did he even still want her as he had during the weeks before the ritual? He gave no sign of that ravenous hunger for her that had resulted in their first night together last month. If he did not want her, would she have anything else to bargain with?

Yes, she had one more thing to offer. She realized after listening to Haakon that there was one other thing Gavin needed that no one else could provide to him—the truth of his origins.

Though she did not know much more than he did, Godrod had traveled far with her father and told her of stone circles on some of the western isles and in the west of Scotland. After their experience that day in the stone circle near Durness, she suspected there might be a connection between the stones and his power. Without proof she could not say definitely, but Godrod, who could speak the language of the Scots, promised to find out more when they arrived in Dunfermline or in Dun Eidann, the large and growing city on the other side of the firth.

Gavin shifted beneath her hands, bringing her attention back to him. He leaned forward, giving her access to his lower back. Another bucket of water stood next to the tub, so she lifted it and wet his hair to wash it. Long accustomed to seeing to the hospitality of her father's houseguests, Katla quickly and efficiently cleaned him, wincing when she encountered the lump on the back of his head where he'd been struck.

He put up with her ministrations silently, not saying another word or acknowledging her touch as she worked. For her part, Katla tried to ignore the feel of his skin, knowing that she'd kissed and tasted most every inch of his body. She tried to ignore the way his muscles tensed, remembering the strength of them when he held her up and wrapped her legs around his waist. And she tried to ignore the wanting and desire curling deep within her own body as she watched him stand before her.

His cock stood rampant only inches away from her mouth and she forced herself to remain unmoving. Just the thought of taking it in her mouth and suckling on it made her body ache. A wetness grew between her legs. Katla wanted him even knowing that nothing was settled between them. Even knowing he might leave her behind. Even knowing the risks to her heart, she wanted to feel him within her, touching her as deeply as a man could.

She did not take her eyes from his cock as she scooped more soap in her shaking hands and smoothed it over his legs, moving higher and higher. His inward-drawn, hissing breath as she skimmed over it to clean his hips and stomach encouraged her.

He was not immune to her touch. He wanted her as much as she wanted him. Before talk of bargains and agreements, they were just man and woman.

She slid her hands around his cock, grasping it as a man would take a sword in his hands, and lathered the length of it. When she dared a glance at his face, Gavin closed his eyes, dropped his head back, and let out a moan of pleasure. Feeling the power of his arousal, she caressed his cock, sliding her hands around and under the sac and massaging it gently. Deciding she would take his cock in her mouth, she lifted up the bucket and rinsed the soap from it. But before she could pleasure him in that way, he stopped her.

"This changes nothing, Katla."

There was much to say and much to settle between them. She did not bother to reply because she knew his ears would not hear her words. Instead, she leaned forward and touched the tip of her tongue to the head of his cock. Sliding her fingers around it, she stroked it, her tongue gliding over the skin as her hands caressed the length. He allowed it for only a few moments and then stepped back.

"Your gown is going to get wet," he murmured in a voice husky with arousal and need. "Take it off."

Her body ached now at the thought of joining with him. The knowledge of the pleasure he would bring her forced a shudder that shook her to her core. The tips of her breasts tightened and more wetness gathered between her legs. She fumbled with the clasp of the brooches that held her tunic in place, unable to unhook them. Wasting no time, Gavin reached over, took all the layers she wore in his hands, and pulled them over her head. Naked and shivering with need, she stood before him as his gaze burned her skin with its intensity and desire.

After tossing her garments aside, he stepped from the tub and stalked toward her. She could still have resisted, but he lifted his head up and closed his eyes for a moment, sniffing the air around them as though searching for a scent. Katla breathed in his musky smell, and it awakened some primitive need within her, increasing the desire that pulsed through her blood in anticipation of his first touch.

She arched, her breasts swelling with need, her core throbbing and wet for him. That he could not hear her words at least saved her from the humiliation of admitting that need to him aloud. The first touch of his body and hers came in a most unexpected way, for nothing but their lips met. Far gentler than she imagined it could be, he covered her mouth with his, teasing the line of her lips until she opened to let him in.

Then it was a like a storm erupting around them; the air seemed charged and filled with excitement and arousal. He wrapped himself around her, lifting her and walking her back to the pallet in the corner, where he took her down and spread her legs with his body. He entered her with such power that it was her turn to gasp. Then, she could think no more, for her body took over and simply felt his every touch.

The last cohesive thought that flitted through her mind was that he was wrong.

This time, this joining of their flesh and souls, changed everything.

Chapter Nineteen

He'd wanted to refuse her.
He'd wanted to ignore her.
He wanted . . . her.

If she had simply shaken her head, refusing his demand for her to take off her clothes, he would have controlled the raging beast within him. Even as her body and her soul began to sing to him, breaking into the damned silence of his mind with sounds that tempted him from one kind of madness to another, he wanted to walk away.

She'd had him kidnapped!

She'd ignored his words and his warnings and gone off on her own path.

She infuriated him.

The moment she fumbled around with the brooches holding her clothing in place and beseeched him with eyes filled with the same wanting he felt, Gavin gave in. But he did not move until the moment her body reacted to being naked before him and he saw the shiver that passed through her. Then he lost control.

He took her.

Gavin had made no attempt to spread out their pleasure, to

make it last, to make her come over and over until she passed out from too much pleasure. No, not this time, when his anger at her pulsed so brightly and while the sounds of her blood and body excited him to new heights of desire. This time he took her, filling her so quickly, so powerfully, so deeply that she spasmed around his prick the moment he thrust inside her.

Their bodies had barely hit the pallet when she arched against him, wrapping her arms around his back and her legs around his waist, pulling him in and keeping him there with her strong inner muscles. Like an untried boy, his body burned as he spilled his seed deep within her, in endless ripples of pleasure while she screamed out her release and he his.

He'd been so wrong. In spite of the haste of this coupling, in spite of his anger at her and his claim that it changed nothing, a slight twinge in his heart told him that much had changed. Gavin heard sounds from deep within her that were not of her body's making. This time, he'd heard a whisper of her thoughts and the echoes of her soul. And it scared him to think that she was becoming part of him.

Especially now that his end was within months.

It took him a long time to recover from their joining. He listened as her heart slowed to its regular pace and her blood cooled and her body relaxed. When those sounds faded in his mind, he fell back into the depths of silence. Eight days had passed since the ritual and his deafness remained. How many more days until it passed from him?

He lifted his weight off her and moved to her side. Katla lay with her eyes closed but that did not stop the tear from rolling down her face. Had he hurt her? Gavin leaned up on one elbow and traced its path.

"I did not mean to hurt you," he whispered. He caressed her cheek with his finger. "I am sorry if I did." She shook her head but would not meet his gaze. Hel!

'Twas time for the truth between them.

"I cannot hear for days and days after the ritual, Katla. Even now I remain as deaf as one born without hearing."

He tried to keep his voice level, a difficult task when he could not hear the sound of it himself. She opened her eyes and met his gaze. Her mouth moved but he could not hear the words she spoke.

"I cannot hear you. I will not hear you for a few more days, so explaining this"—he nodded at the chamber around them— "or anything else will do no good now."

He thought she might leave then, but she did not. It had been more than a week since he'd held her in his embrace and that long since he'd slept well. In a short time, he felt sleep tugging him down into its grasp.

When he awoke she was gone, and like the first time, he wondered if he'd dreamed her presence. He tugged on the clean clothes left for him and went to the door of the small cottage. It did not open when he pulled on it. He only banged on it once before understanding that he was yet her prisoner and that only his prison had changed.

Katla walked from the small cottage back to the shore. The men stayed there, as ordered, to give her some measure of privacy as she met with Gavin. They thought she meant to speak to him, but she'd known her true intent when she'd ordered the cottage to be prepared and furnished. If Godrod disapproved, he did not show it, accepting her directions without comment or questioning glance.

Walking helped ease some of the soreness from her limbs. Being on the ship for days, without space to walk, had made her legs ache. Once on land here in Caithness, she'd done little more than walk to the cottage. Now, walking helped to stretch her legs. She tried to collect her thoughts before reaching the camp the men had set up near the beach. Half of them remained behind on the ship, the other half here.

"He did not hurt you," Godrod said as she approached him. Katla tried not to blush as she remembered Gavin's words about the same thing, but heat crept up her cheeks. "He did not," she said quietly, nodding to a place away from the others so that they could speak privately.

They reached a small clearing and stopped.

"There is more than one way to hurt a woman, Katla," Godrod said softly.

"I am well, Godrod," she said, not meeting his astute gaze.

"Can he hear you yet?"

She'd shared the knowledge she had about the Truthsayer with Godrod. If he was to be of any help, he needed to know what they faced.

"Nay. From what Haakon said, it will be days more before his hearing returns." She fisted her hands and groaned out her frustration. "I cannot wait more days, Godrod. Kali's life grows more endangered with each passing day."

"Harald is there to protect Kali, child." Godrod shook his head. "If there is no pressing reason for the king to take action against your brother, he will not."

Katla considered his words. She needed to convince Gavin to come peacefully, for his opposition could result in harming him and she wanted no part of that. Watching him forcibly taken had been a terrible assault on her heart, one she would not recover from for a long time. She had no desire to be the cause of something worse.

"Two days," she said. "If he cannot hear, we will begin our journey and sail southward until he does."

"It might be safer if you did not return to him until we can speak to him, Katla."

"He will not hurt me, Godrod. He could have earlier but did not."

"You have much faith in someone you have known for such a short time," he warned. "Have a care."

Considering herself warned, Katla decided to heed his words for now and sleep in a tent where the others slept. She would see Gavin again the morning.

The sun's light pouring in through a small opening in the cottage wall told him it was day. He'd slept better than he had in days—sated by food and Katla. Gavin knew she would return, but not when, so he sat on the pallet with his back to the wall. She would not sneak in without his seeing her.

She was so desperate to save her brother that she was not thinking clearly now. He could not blame her for that. He had imagined having brothers when he was a child and knew if he'd had any, he would fight the forces of hell to protect them. If he'd had any. . . .

But, he would not be the one to help her this time.

She would need to rely on Harald's skills as the representative of Earl Magnus to convince the king to release the boy. No otherworldly talent was needed here—only an experienced negotiator, and Harald was such a man. If Harald became more appealing in Katla's eyes because he'd bargained for her brother's life, well, so be it.

He could be no further help to her, for traveling so close to so many would be too painful to bear.

By the time she finally opened the door and entered, he had all his arguments ready to present. All the reasons why it would not work, how he would not be able to sort through the clamor during the weeks before the next full moon, how he had never faced so many people in such a small area before, and on and on.

Gavin stood and stretched, tired of being imprisoned. He wanted to walk; he wanted to sit in the sun. He wanted to have this settled between them so he could return to Durness.

When the door finally opened, he welcomed the chance to speak to her. So when he faced her old servant Godrod, who wore his suspicions and mistrust on his face, Gavin was disappointed.

"Where is your mistress?" he asked.

The old man pointed outside without saying a word. Ah, he knew.

"Tell her I wish to speak with her."

Godrod crossed his arms over his chest and stepped aside, allowing Katla entrance. The man had no intention of letting his mistress in here alone again—that much was clear from his stance. Did he think Gavin would harm her? Again, clearly he must.

"I would speak to you without your servant present, Katla."

Katla faced Godrod and they spoke, sparing him a glance or two during their heated conversation. Finally, Katla must have prevailed, for the man glared at her and then at him and left abruptly, slamming the door so hard Gavin felt the frame shake.

"So you have that effect on others, Katla? 'Tis not just me?" he asked.

The corner of her mouth threatened a smile, but she controlled it at the last moment and glared at him. He watched her mouth move but could not hear her words. He clapped his hands over his head and groaned out in frustration.

"It lasts longer each month. It could be days more before I can hear you." Gavin met her gaze. "You must release me, Katla, and allow me to return to Durness."

She pressed her lips together tightly, forming a line of refusal. He walked over and took her by the shoulders.

"Did Haakon tell you why I dare not go near a place like Dunfermline? Why even Birsay is a threat to me?"

He did not expect an answer, so he continued. He would tell her what she needed to know now. Let her think on response until they could discuss it. He released her before continuing, walking across the small space to the other side.

"Over these last months, as the power has grown, so too have the aftereffects, Katla. The noise in my head grows stronger and more painful. One of the things that seems to affect the pain are the number of people around me. You know that. I explained it to you. But what I didn't explain is that the more people around me, the more pain I have."

She moved toward him, but he stopped her with a wave of his hand. "A city like Dunfermline will be too much for me to bear, Katla. Even with the control you seem to give me, there are thousands of inhabitants in that area whose thoughts will invade my mind. I will go mad."

She paled at his words, but worse, he witnessed disappointment in her gaze. Disappointment in him. He could not bear that either.

"You ask too much of me, Katla. I am only a man."

She shook her head and he did not need to hear her words to understand what she said.

You are not a man—you are the Truthsayer.

He shook his head. "Nay, Katla. I am only a man."

When she set her chin in that stubborn way, he knew he was in trouble. She was now determined to change his mind. Knowing he could not hear her, she turned from him and walked out of the cottage, still wearing that expression that spoke of unwavering purpose. He thought to follow her, but Godrod stepped in front of the door, blocking his path.

"Godrod, leave the door open. I will not try to leave," he said. After too many days closed up, he wanted to feel the air on his skin. If it meant agreeing not to escape—for now—he would give his word. It would not bind him once his hearing returned, but for now . . .

The old man looked off to his left and when satisfied with

the answer Katla gave, he nodded to Gavin, pulling the door open. One battle won but far too many left to fight, he thought as he settled back on the pallet to get more sleep.

Their truce held for three days. During that time, Katla appeared every few hours bringing food to him. Sometimes she left it for him to eat alone, and other times she remained and shared it with him. They allowed him to walk in a small area around the cottage, under guard, but it was enough for him to stretch his legs. Godrod stood nearby whenever he left the cottage and usually positioned himself between Gavin and Katla.

Gavin knew she was dying to speak her mind to him. He suspected he actually had little choice in what was to come—only in the manner in which it happened.

Chapter Twenty

The day dawned rainy and cold, as many did in autumn, when the warm days of summer became memories only. The waters offshore would soon be rough and stormy as September peaked and the colors of the season changed from the brilliant hues of summer to the bleak shades of winter. As close as Gavin could tell, the next full moon would come in the very first days of October, followed by another one at the end of the month. Not a usual occurrence, and some would say, a dire portent of things to come.

The air carried a sound to him like a whisper or an echo, and at first he thought he was hearing thoughts. Then it became stronger and he recognized her voice, speaking somewhere nearby. Gavin walked to the doorway and looked out. Sure enough, Katla stood not ten paces away, under the cover of a copse of tall trees, talking with two men he did not know. Neither they nor Katla herself noticed him watching, so he stayed and listened.

"The ship is ready, mistress," the taller one said.

"Once this weather clears, we should sail," the other said. "If the storms come early, it could add another week to our voyage."

"Do we head north or south, mistress?" Gavin asked, mimicking the respectful tone of the other two.

"Get Godrod," she said, dismissing them and walking toward him.

He met her halfway. She stared at him for a moment and then nodded.

"You can hear me," she said.

He nodded in reply. "You did not answer me—do you head north or south?"

Katla tried to walk past him, but he grabbed her by the arm. Godrod ran to her side and pushed him away. When he would have fought back, Katla stepped between them.

"May we speak in private, Gavin?" She looked at the older man. "Godrod, all is well. Prepare to sail."

He would have disagreed with her, but it mattered not what was said about a voyage south—he would not, could not go. Once Godrod stood aside, Gavin followed Katla into the small chamber and pulled the door closed behind him.

Anger seethed in the air between them. All the words he'd wanted to say and hear for the last two weeks welled up inside.

"Why?" He spat the words out.

It hung in the air for several moments as she tried to gather her voice and her courage to speak. All the words she'd practiced over these last days disappeared.

"I have told you my reason for not being able to go to the city with you, and yet you still plan to take me there. If I speak out against you, I can have you imprisoned as you have done with me this last week, but with no release in sight."

Her throat went dry at his threat. He could have her arrested and worse. His position with Earl Magnus would be known in Dunfermline. Her attempts to bring him south against his will would be exposed and punished.

"Do you really want to risk taking me there, Katla? Will

these men follow your orders when they know the risk?" He walked toward her, and she backed up a step or two as he did. His reaction was not what she'd expected, but then a cornered animal is always the most dangerous one.

"I have a bargain to offer you, Truthsayer," she said, trying to calm his temper. Instead it seemed to anger him more.

"So, it comes down to a bargain?" He rubbed his face and shook his head. "I thought there was something else between us. Even though you denied it on the day we returned from Durness, I felt it, Katla."

She wanted to cry. She wished that she could go back in time to a year ago when she lived a happy life and had no worries like the ones she faced now. She wished she had not begun to fall in love with this man.

Katla shuddered as the truth of her realization seeped into her soul and her heart. Though she'd always wished to fall in love, she'd thought it would bring her joy. Not like this, having to bargain her body away once more and tear her heart out to persuade this man to help her.

"Was the other day just a sampling of the wares so I would be tempted to accept whatever you offered me?"

She gasped at his insult. "The other day . . . the other day . . ." she began but could not finish. She wanted to tell him of her feelings, but his anger prevented her from revealing such things. "You are angry."

"The hel I am!" he said. "You lured me from the earl's house and had men kidnap me. You dragged me here, to . . ."

"Caithness," she answered.

"Caithness. I beg you, stop this now. Accept that I would help you if I could." He let out a long, exhausted breath. "I would help if I thought I could survive it. There will be too many people to hold back from my mind. Too many." His voice lowered then, and she heard the terror there. "I will go mad."

"I will help you control the madness," she offered. "Whatever you need, I will be there."

His expression grew bleak, and he shook his head. "I do not know if even you have the power to help me control the assault of thousands of minds, Katla. In Durness, even in Birsay, there were few compared to those I will encounter if I go to Dunfermline."

She sensed a change in him—from complete opposition to something less inflexible. But she felt the fear that filled every part of him, too. She reached out and took his hand in hers.

"I will be at your side the whole time, Gavin. We can find a way to battle the clamor. We can do this together."

"And then what will happen? If your brother is proven innocent, will you return with him to Orkney? And if he is guilty, where will you go?"

She shrugged. "I cannot think that far ahead, Gavin. I can only do everything in my power to prove his innocence."

"In all this time, Katla, have you ever asked your brother about his knowledge of your father's plot? Has he spoken to you about this at all?"

She paused, realizing that the only subject she and Kali spoke about when Harald held him prisoner was her attempts to free him. Kali never answered her questions. When she asked about the plot, he changed the topic, never quite explaining why others would suspect him of complicity. "No."

"Mayhap that should be a warning to you? Mayhap you should step back and reconsider this path?" Gavin shook his head. "Allow Harald to do what he can, and then let your brother determine his own fate."

All she could hear in that moment was her father's voice, demanding, begging her to intervene and to save her brother. Katla needed to convince Gavin to help her. "If not for me, Gavin, then do this for yourself."

Her words stopped him cold. He could see and hear her utter desperation.

"For myself?" he asked. "What can I possibly gain?"

"I sent Godrod in search of knowledge about your powers and your family. I can tell you what he found. . . ." She let her words drift off.

He wanted to deny the power of those words, to himself, to her, but his heart beat wildly at the suggestion that she might have information about his past and the powers he had. It was a ploy. A desperate ploy to gain his cooperation. And damn his soul and hers, he wanted to!

"What have you found out?" he asked. "How? Did he find someone who knew my real parents?"

Did Katla know something that could save him from the end he thought nearly in sight? Did anyone else have powers like his? Had his parents . . . He choked back the consuming need to know something about who and what he truly was.

And in that moment, he understood a bit more about the force that drove Katla to protect her brother despite all opposition.

Family. Belonging. Loyalty. Love. None of it was based on truth or lies. All of it was based on uncontrollable, unpredictable, undeniable emotions.

"So you will withhold what you know unless I help you?"

He wanted to be angry, but she had offered him the one, nay two, things he needed most—the physical relationship with her that would calm the insanity in his mind, and the promise of knowledge about his origins. While he'd lain insensate in the aftermath of using his powers, she'd been planning, searching, and finding a way to gain his compliance.

She was truly Sven's daughter, showing every sign of the keen mind and relentless determination her father had been known for. He would have been proud of her.

"I will offer you all my help both before the next ritual and after it," she replied. "To control the chaos and to find your origins," she promised.

As much as he'd like to call her bluff and demand proof of what she'd learned, his heart soared at the possibility she was telling the truth. He held out his right hand to her to accept her bargain. When she placed her hand in his, a shock passed through him, and he wondered about the meaning of it. She'd felt it, too, but she did not let go.

"I accept your bargain," he said.

"And I yours," she replied.

To remind her what her part was, Gavin pulled her to him, still holding her right hand, while sliding his left one into her hair and bringing her face to his.

"At my side," he whispered, kissing her mouth. "In my bed until this ends," he added as he nipped the skin of her neck until she shuddered and her body began to throb with a need he could hear. "Under my hand at all times," he added.

He planned to seal their bargain in a most primitive and elementary way. Sliding his hand down her body and grasping the edge of her tunic, he lifted it to expose her legs to him. She gasped against his mouth as he touched the damp curls and then slid his finger into her cleft. Her entire body shuddered as her nether folds swelled under his touch. Soon, she arched against his fingers, riding his hand much like she had his prick.

It took only minutes to bring her to satisfaction, and though he had not reached his, he was at peace with that, for the voyage to Dunfermline would take another week. She would be his at all times and that knowledge pleased him.

Gavin only hoped against all hope that whatever made her different would keep the clamor at bay. Or he would face his last months sunken into madness and chaos.

Chapter Twenty-one

The next days aboard ship traveling south were not the hardship that the first ones had been. Once Gavin had consented to accompany her to the city of the Scottish king, everything changed.

The small chamber where Gavin had been held prisoner was cleaned and a pallet and some other furnishings returned to it. Though they both spent much time on the upper deck as they sailed the miles of open sea, the chamber became their hideaway from the world . . . and their future it seemed. They filled their nights with passion and Katla was surprised by his unbridled need for her. Sometimes she would catch a glimpse of terror in his gaze, but joining with him seemed to banish it.

Now, a week later, Katla blushed at his latest suggestion and then agreed as she always did. The bargain had faded away, replaced by his honest desire for her . . . and by something else that grew with each passing day and each long conversation between them.

The day when he'd revealed his dangerous thoughts about having her tied up as he'd been and taking her from behind had ended with that exact scenario between them. Instead of tying her hands behind her back, he'd tied them in front of her and then knotted that rope around the beam above that supported the upper deck. He'd peeled off her clothes, piece by piece, until she stood there naked and wanting. Kneeling between her legs, he licked and suckled until she begged for release.

Instead of guiding her leg around his waist as he usually did when they coupled standing up, he walked around behind her and played with her from there. With hands between her legs, he made her wet and then spread that moisture over her cleft until he could slide his cock along it easily. He pressed on the small bud between her legs, rubbing it, stroking it, and then he eased himself between the globes of her bottom and into the puckered opening there.

He moved slowly at first, waiting for her body to adjust to such an invasion. When he was seated deep, he pulled the rope free and bent her forward to give himself better access and entry.

Katla could not believe the intensity of it. With his cock deep in one opening and his fingers teasing the other, it took but a few deep strokes to bring her release. He held onto her hips then, thrusting deeper still into that tight channel, not slowing because of her release, but relentlessly filling her over and over until she peaked again . . . Then he spilled his seed.

He guided her to her knees and held her close until their bodies calmed. Then he eased out of her and soothed the opening with his fingers. She'd had no idea that a man and woman could join in such a manner.

But he was teaching her new pleasures all the time. He waited now for her to initiate things with a touch or a kiss, and then he plowed her deeply and well in a variety of positions that she'd never dreamed of. He did not force her to do anything she did not wish. Gavin let her be the first to indicate willingness.

Even now, he smiled at her surprise and then waited for her

to become accustomed to the idea of mutual pleasuring each other in a different way. Her blood heated and her skin tingled as he described in a low, tempting tone how they could accomplish such an act. By the time his words stopped, she lay panting and awaiting the touch of his mouth and the caress of his hands where she ached most.

This time the scandalous suggestion involved him suckling between her legs while she suckled his cock. Uncertain of how it could be accomplished, she allowed him to guide her to it. Within a short but completely pleasurable time Katla lay replete in his arms.

Then the other sensation happened again.

A wave of tremors hit her, not like the ones during bedplay when her body shuddered in release. These tremors were unpleasant and pulled her from the lethargic aftermath of pleasure, making her restless, nervous. When she glanced over at Gavin, she knew he was feeling them, too.

"Gavin?" She turned on her side to find him pale. "What is it?" she asked.

"The noise," was all he could say.

She held him close, stroking his arm and hoping her nearness would help. Gavin pressed his head against her breasts and seemed to breathe in time with the beating of her heart. It soothed him somehow and he soon fell asleep.

The closer they got to Dunfermline, the more often those tremors occurred, and Katla realized that somehow she was bound to what he felt. And he was being battered with each mile they journeyed closer to the Scottish city and Kali's destiny.

Godrod left the ship as soon as they docked, but Gavin remained below deck until they could contact Harald and arrangements could be made for their stay. The firth and the ports along it bustled with merchant ships and every other kind as befitted the area where the royal palace and the abbey favored by the previous queen both stood. Across the firth, another city grew on the top of an old mountain, though no one believed it would ever rival the prestige of Dunfermline. Finally word came from Harald that lodgings had been secured for them near the palace, and they traveled there on horseback with a wagon carrying their clothing. They were taken to their chambers when they arrived, and Harald warned them to remain within, drawing no attention to themselves or to Gavin's reputation or powers. Kali was being held somewhere within the grounds of the monastery, but he was not allowed visitors.

Days passed and Katla spent most of her time with Gavin. Though they passed many hours in pleasurable bedplay, they also talked about their lives and about those of the people she'd met in Durness. As the moon waxed, Gavin became noticeably more fitful in his sleep and tense when awake.

Then, finally, the king arrived back in Dunfermline and the day of the full moon approached. Soon no amount of physical release eased the tension within either of them and for the first time, Katla feared the worst.

Gavin paced the confines of the chamber, bigger than the one in Caithness but much smaller than his room in Birsay. The days grew shorter as autumn approached, but each night the moon's light grew brighter as it moved closer to full. He felt the changes more than he had at any time since Katla had entered his life. Even she could not lessen the chaos and pain created by so many people so close by.

Not that she did not try. He smiled thinking on her enthusiasm as they shared a bed since they'd left Caithness.

They often passed the time playing boardgames he'd learned at the earl's court. They talked for endless hours, especially when the chaos threatened him and his head ached with it. If he thought on the sounds of her body at those times, the pain did ease, but it seemed to return quicker than ever before.

He learned much about her during those quiet times. How her keen mind worked to solve problems. How deeply she felt about her family. How fragile she was in spite of the appearance of strength she presented. It was this last realization that led him once more to his friend Harald, who had made himself scarce during this time. They met the day before the moon would reach its fullness because Gavin wanted arrangements to be made for Katla's safety in case he did not survive the ritual or Kali was found guilty.

When Gavin turned into the small walkway that led to the monastery's chapel, Harald stood waiting for him. They walked together in silence for a few minutes before either one was ready to discuss the terrible possibilities ahead for Katla's brother.

"You have enough men for this, Harald?" he asked after Harald explained his plan. "The king's steward will not be suspicious of the number?"

Harald's decision to have several men ready to spirit Katla out of the chamber after the ritual seemed sound, as long as they were not obvious. Harald pointed to places on a crude drawing of the chamber where the ritual would occur.

"As long as none approach Kali, there will be no objections. The king's men understand that there must be witnesses to whatever is said."

Gavin waited until several monks walked past them before continuing with his questions. "The journey to Orkney?"

"You need not know the details, Gavin. She will be safe," Harald said. "What will you do?"

"Haakon has arrived and will see to me after the ritual. Once I can travel, or before that if things go badly, he will make certain I get back to Durness."

The silence grew between them until finally Harald asked the question that had plagued them both.

"Do you truly believe your end is near, Gavin?"

"My heart slows with each ritual, beginning anew after a longer and longer pause. I fear that it will not beat again if that pause is too long. I believe that time will come at the next ritual."

"Next one? At the end of the month?" his friend asked.

"Aye. The one that coincides with the anniversary of my birth. Ironic is it not, to die on the day you were born?"

Harald did not quip lightly about so serious a subject, even though death was familiar to a warrior such as he. "And there is nothing you can do? No one who knows about this power of yours?"

"Katla says she does."

"How would she know such a thing?" Harald scoffed.

"She said Godrod has discovered knowledge about me that she will share once I speak Kali's truth," he explained.

"If such knowledge could be found, Magnus's men would have uncovered it years ago. I believe she would say anything to gain your aid." Harald stared at him and shook his head.

"You told me once that I should have said the words. Now I challenge you to do the same."

"I cannot, Harald. If what I suspect is true, I will be dead before the month is out."

Harald gathered up the scrap of paper with the map of the chamber on it and tucked it in a sack he wore tied to his belt. "Does she know? That you believe you will die because of the ritual? Did she ask this of you knowing it could hasten your death?"

Gavin shook his head. "I did not tell her. She knows all but that part of it. With Kali to fret and grieve over, she does not need something else drawing her attention."

"Do you know what the worst part of this is?" Harald asked.

"Tell me," Gavin said, not believing there could be much that was worse than their inadvertent—and sometimes deliberate—actions, which had led to her father's death. They stopped and Gavin waited for the answer.

"The earl would not have demanded Kali's death. We spoke before he left with the king. He was planning to exile the boy, not put him to death."

"Do you jest, Harald?" Gavin asked. "Does Katla know?"

"Nay, but there is more."

"Tell me now. Delay no more in this," Gavin warned him.

"The only reason Kali faces death now is because Katla raised the matter so publicly. Once it came to the attention of the two kings, the earl could no longer handle justice in his own manner."

Gavin lost his balance and tripped then, falling hard against the wall next to him. "How did it come to that?"

"Her uncle appealed to the king after she spoke at the ritual. He wanted them both executed, but there has been no question raised of her involvement, only Kali's. So to appease Olaf, the king sent Kali here to face judgment."

"Though you said my words proved Olaf trustworthy, I have no liking for a man who pursues the death of his kin in such a manner," Gavin said.

"Aye," Harald agreed. "And one who manages to get others to do the deed for him."

The sound of footsteps on the other side of the wall startled them both. "Come," Harald said. "There is much to be set in place before the ritual."

Katla stumbled away, barely able to stand or walk. She'd gone looking for Harald with a question, and one of the servants had told her to seek him here, in the yard between the palace and the monastery. Having taken the wrong corridor, she searched but could not find them until she heard their muffled voices speaking and spotted their heads above a garden wall.

About to call out to them, she'd been stunned into silence by the words she heard.

If Kali died, it would be her fault.

Her stomach rebelled at such a thing and she fell to her knees on the ground. When the spasms ceased, she was weak and horrified at the truth.

If she'd simply lived with Harald and kept quiet, Kali would be safe.

If she'd been obedient and listened instead of believing herself always right, Kali would be exiled, but alive and not facing execution.

When she raised her head, she was so confused that she could not face anyone. It took hours to regain control before she could face either Harald or Gavin. And that night she sought oblivion when she joined with Gavin, asking him to pour out his scent so she could lose herself of the pain of this discovery. If he thought it strange that she wanted him to do the one thing that set her apart from the other women he'd had, he said nothing.

And for a few minutes that night, she forgot everything that caused such pain in her heart and allowed the pleasure he could create when he ensorcelled her body to control her.

Chapter Twenty-two

The abbott of Dunfermline monastery wanted no part of what he called an "unholy thing." He was certain the truthspeaking was an abomination and evil in the sight of God. Harald had shown his intelligence by bringing with him the abbott from the monastery on the Brough of Birsay, who declared that Gavin had held the holy relics of their church and not been burned by them—as any sinner or abomination would have been. After several hours of discussion, the king's intervention, and a large donation, the ritual was set to be held in a private chamber of the royal palace next to the monastery's lands.

The power had grown again, Gavin could feel the surges of it within him, and he could hear the thoughts of some in the room even without touching. He paced the chamber, feeling it heat his blood and make his heart race. He searched for Katla and found her, standing in the corner near Harald. Though he wanted to tell her everything would be fine, he feared he knew what the outcome would be. At least his friend would be there to help Katla through what would happen.

Kali stood closest to him now, next to a chair they'd placed in the front of the room. King Edgar's witnesses stood close as well. The king would not be present, for though this matter had been brought to his attention, it was not important enough to require his royal presence. The monks offered a prayer and left, not at ease with these proceedings. The witnesses had been told of the ritual and knew what to expect, but that rarely prepared anyone who observed it for the first time.

When Gavin could no longer contain the flow of it, he walked to the seat and took his place. This time he would try to stay awake as the truthspeaking happened so that he could guide the ritual. But despite Gavin's resolve, the last thing he remembered was the terror in Katla's eyes as she watched him take Kali's hand in his.

Harald had men spread throughout the chamber, but if the worst happened, there would be nothing he could do. And the tightness in his gut told him to prepare for just that. Katla trembled at his side, grasping his cloak like a child seeking comfort. In many ways she was just that—now orphaned, abandoned by her uncle, and about to lose the only other family she had.

"Harald," she whispered, tugging on his hand, "Tell him to stop." Her face paled and her eyes widened in desperation. "I was wrong to ask for this."

Her admission, surprising as it was, came too late to save her brother now. If only she'd not pursued this. . . .

"Too late," he whispered back, shaking his head. " 'Tis too late, Katla."

The king, having been forced to this by the earl of Orkney, would dispense justice swiftly, he'd been told. Harald understood his displeasure at having his judgment questioned, but Edgar had acquiesced in anticipation of future benefits from granting the earl, his neighbor to the north, this small gesture of friendship. Assured that punishment was his to determine, the Scots king had allowed the earl's truthsayer to be called.

Harald watched as Gavin sat in the chair provided and began to change before their eyes. If Harald watched this a hundred more times, he would never easily accept what he saw. His mind rebelled at the sight of his friend changing into someone, or something, else and then entering the mind and memories of another. There was a moment during the ritual he'd undergone when their thoughts were joined and he could hear the pain and confusion within Gavin. Once the questions began though, he could think of nothing else. And he remembered giving answers without hesitation, feeling compelled by the force of Gavin's mind over his own. His thoughts, his mind, did the bidding of another.

As Kali would in just moments.

Katla stiffened next to him, and he took her hand in his. He wondered whether the feelings that existed between her and Gavin would be destroyed when she heard him prove her brother guilty of treason against the earl and the king. It would shock her, but he sensed a deep emotional connection between Gavin and Katla that he suspected would never be broken in life.

No matter what, he accepted that she would never be his in the way he wanted her to be. Oh, he did not doubt she would honor their agreement and return to him, but her heart had been given and would remain forever with his friend.

If what Gavin feared came to pass, Harald would take her back. In his household, as his mistress, she would be protected. And with the passing of time, she might even come to have some tender feelings for him. He could be content with that and honor his pledge to Gavin to see to her welfare when he was gone.

Gavin's voice called out, asking who summoned the Truthsayer, and Kali answered, his voice shaking. Was it fear or guilt that caused his trembling?

"I am Kali Svenson," he said.

"I am Kali Svenson," Gavin repeated in the voice of someone else.

"I am Kali Svenson," they said in one voice that was neither but both at the same time. Chills ran down Harald's spine at the unnatural sound.

The king's minister asked the first question about Kali's knowledge of his father's plotting, and he damned himself from his first word. Question after question revealed that the son was as integral to the plans as the father. Harald's heart hurt for Katla, and when he dared to look at her, he saw her shock and horror at being confronted by the truth.

The king's soldiers moved to surround Kali even before the questions ended, and Harald knew he must get Katla out of the chamber before they took her brother. Once the shock wore off, she would take action, and he would be hard pressed to control her or guarantee her safety. If the king's soldiers thought her involved, her life could be forfeit as well.

Harald nodded to his men and caught Haakon's eye, giving him the signal they'd agreed upon earlier. With one arm around her shoulders and the other placed hastily over her mouth, Harald dragged her from the chamber and down the long corridor to the steps. Running and half carrying her, he did not stop until they were out of the palace and across the yard to where the rest of his men and their horses awaited. With a nod to those already mounted, he tossed Katla onto the horse, climbed up behind her, and rode to the cottage on the outskirts of Dunfermline where he'd arranged to stay the night.

Through it all she said not a word. She stared off as though watching something in the distance. Hours later, the man who'd remained behind caught up with them and delivered the news.

Kali Svenson had been beheaded at Dunfermline Palace within minutes of the ritual's end. Gavin had delivered the truth, and Edgar had delivered swift justice.

Harald did not tell her. The rational part of her knew it already, and he was afraid that saying the words would destroy the fragile control she had over herself. She ate nothing, said nothing, and moved not at all once he sat her in the chair in the cottage. No words he spoke to her brought any response or reply or even a glance in his direction. She resisted when he tried to move her to the bed, so he left her as she sat and covered her with several thick blankets.

The other men slept outside, but he would stay inside and see to her during the night. He'd only intended to rest on the bed, but when he opened his eyes, he discovered her gone from the cottage. Believing that she sought to relieve herself outside, he went in search of her. An hour later, after they'd searched the entire area around the cottage, Harald had to accept that she was gone . . . and he feared he knew where she'd gone. Without knowledge of the roads, Harald had to wait until morning to return to the palace in Dunfermline.

The next day's search for her was unsuccessful, and Harald was faced with few choices. Finding her among the Scots would be nearly impossible. He and his men were strangers here and knew little of the area. If anyone gave them any help, it would surprise him.

The only thing he could do would be to ask the help of the Scots king, and the earl had fobidden him to do that exact thing. This incident had caused problems for Earl Magnus and his king at a time when the new treaty between the Norse and the Scots was shaky at best. Bringing more attention to Sven Rognvaldson and his family would cause trouble that neither Magnus the King nor Magnus the Earl wanted at their door.

Harald made his way back to the palace and called on Haakon to find out Gavin's condition and whether he had any knowledge of Katla's plans. The ever-efficient servant could tell him nothing, and the lady's own servant had disappeared, too.

Harald had never felt so useless—the two people he most cared about were in trouble and mayhap in danger, and he could help neither of them. Not willing to give up yet, he left word with Haakon for Gavin to seek him out once he'd recovered from the ritual.

Riding back to the croft, he tried to come up with other ways to find Katla and get her safely home. They could make other decisions once she was safe.

Gavin struggled against the pain. Though his ears hurt, it was in a strange and different way from the months before, almost a freezing burn rather than one from heat. He could hear nothing—not the voices of those around him, not the usual sounds of a busy household, not questions asked or words spoken in reply. He lay on a pallet in the small chamber he'd been taken to once the ritual ended, with only Haakon attending him.

In spite of the fear and suspicion of the monks at the abbey, Gavin was treated now as an honored guest, and any request for his comfort was fulfilled with haste. For all the good it did him. Three days passed before he could even rise from the pallet, a fourth day before he could remain upright through his waking hours. Not until the fifth day did he feel as though his mind was clear enough to function.

He waited for the voices to return, wondering how he would control them without Katla nearby. He feared that Kali's would now join the chaos of sound since their thoughts had joined for that time. For two months now, because of Katla, he could control the other thoughts that invaded his mind right after the ritual, even when his strength had been drained by the flow of power and he could do little to protect himself from the onslaught. But Gavin feared the loss of that control and only wondered how long it would take before the last shreds of it slipped out of his grasp completely.

His heart hurt with the realization that in spite of what he owed her and had promised her against his own good sense, he'd destroyed her by destroying her beloved brother. Oh, he could tell himself that he had no control over what truths he heard or whose thoughts he listened to, but he could have warned her about what he did know and what he suspected. In trying to protect her tender heart, he'd destroyed her.

And he could try to comfort himself with the fact that she had broken her promise to him and not helped him discover more about the origins of this terrible power. How she'd lied to him when she'd sworn she would share what knowledge she had with him once he'd saved her brother.

Part of him, his foolish heart most likely, always suspected she had nothing to bargain with but herself. He should have been able to tell she was lying to him, but he was content with having her in his bed, in his life and in his heart, even if it was for a short time. If it meant another day with her, he would believe whatever she told him.

When he'd regained himself just after the ritual, he'd seen Harald dragging her out, seen the stricken expression in her blue eyes as King Edgar's men took her brother. Condemned by Gavin's words, Kali would be executed immediately by the Scots for his involvement in his father's plans. No mercy would be offered or shown to a traitor—other than the quick death Earl Magnus had requested.

Gavin waited for Harald to send word, needing to know she was safe. They'd come to an understanding, he and Harald, for Gavin knew it was time to set Katla free. Fear struck deep in his heart at the thought of not seeing her again, not holding her, not loving her, but she'd been a pawn too long and now deserved a chance at a life of her own. One that Harald had promised to provide for her.

And if Gavin could survive the pain and madness that would surely strike harder than ever with her gone, he would not have to fret much longer. He now believed that he would face his end on the anniversary of his birth. When the other one left him after the ritual and he had regained a sense of himself, he felt the beating of his heart slow once more. So slow, so faint that he could almost not feel it at all and, worse, for a moment, a brief bit of time, his heart had stopped.

He'd noticed it several months ago, but the pain always seemed more important and required all his attention to deal with. Now, her presence, her nearness, her passion, gave him the necessary strength to overpower the pain and hold the voices and the clamor in a stranglehold of his own making.

At least he'd regained his humanity with Katla's help. So many things he'd ignored or left behind in his climb from obscurity to Truthsayer now seemed so much more important because Katla had brought them back into his life and given him the strength he needed to focus on life and living once more.

Farming. He'd forgotten how much enjoyment he received from working a long, hard day in the fields. Cultivating the soil and watching it become fruitful because of that work. Once Katla calmed the torment in his mind, he could spend days free of pain with enough strength to leave his seclusion and to be among people without fear of the overwhelming clamor.

People. Gavin had long given up being around others because of the pain. Because of his need to dull it with strong drink or other remedies. Because he heard voices that no one else could hear and he sometimes reacted to them without thinking.

Hope. He had lived in despair of ever having a normal life,

a wife, or a family. Katla had eased his pain long enough to allow the last flicker of hope in his soul to burst into flame. In spite of his belief that his end was near, she'd given him a glimpse of what he could have had.

Now, he needed to tamp down that hope and release her to live her own life. And he would, for she'd given him new strength and courage to love her enough to let her go now and not force her to watch him die, too.

After he spoke with Harald and knew that Katla was safe with him, Gavin would return to Durness to face the ends of his days.

Gifted.

Cursed.

Alone as he was meant to be.

Chapter Twenty-three

When Katla regained herself from the mindless, grieving woman she became after witnessing her brother condemned to death by the man she loved, she felt nothing. Then her mind and heart filled with such pain over what had happened, how it happened, and worse, her part in it that she could not think in any rational way for days.

She'd left Harald in the middle of the night and wandered through the countryside without sleeping or eating or thinking. It was not until days and nights later that she noticed Godrod trailing her. She hurt too much to speak or acknowledge him, but his presence eased her in some way. He was the last link to her home and life in her father's house.

She'd taken refuge from a storm when he approached her. He offered her something to drink from a skin, and she accepted it and then a bit of coarse bread that stuck in her throat. He did not speak to her even then, which was a good thing. She could not string words together that would make sense and did not have the strength to try. He simply followed her for the next several days until she began the horrible task of thinking through the pain.

One day, a week later, she thought, Godrod began leading

her instead of following, and she allowed it. With no family left, she had few options. Knowing her uncle wanted her dead, Katla did not know where to seek refuge in Orkney. For now, she trailed Godrod, keeping pace with him as they seemed to make their way back to the shoreline. Katla did not know if they were still in Scotland or had crossed back into Caithness.

And she did not care.

All was lost.

Because of her.

Even Gavin would now suffer because of her—she'd dragged him into this situation, she'd forced him to help her with false promises, and now she'd abandoned him at his most vulnerable time to the punishments inflicted by his powerful gift. She'd used him far more than he'd used her—for his use had been of her body, but she'd used up his heart and soul.

It hurt too much to consider her actions against him, so she pushed them away. For hours at a time, she could keep his face from her mind. For hours, she did not remember the passion he'd shown her or the pleasure they'd shared. For hours, she could force her heart to forget the love that burned for him. Then, in a rush, it flooded back, ripping her traitorous heart to shreds in an instant.

Godrod said nothing about anything he'd witnessed. He kept walking through the countryside, over the rolling hills, and through valleys in the midst of harvest time. He spoke to her in few words, usually directions or questions about food or stopping for the night.

Sometimes he would leave in the middle of the night or early in the morning before she rose, but he never explained his actions. When she finally realized that he would reappear with food or supplies, Katla understood. She did not sleep much, merely laying her exhausted body down and waiting for the sun to rise again.

Godrod pushed her on, forcing her to move and to live even when she had no desire to do so. The days grew cooler and damper as they traveled, and soon she needed her cloak against the cold. When she knew that she would continue to live, even if her life was empty now that she had betrayed the man she loved, she asked Godrod the first question.

"Where are you taking me?"

"We head north," he answered, dropping back to walk at her side. "I have friends and thought to seek shelter for the winter with them."

"In Orkney?"

He shook his head. "Nay, Katla. 'Tis not safe for you in Orkney with your uncle seeking your blood."

So, 'twas true then. Her uncle would not be content until Sven Rognvaldson's children were gone. He wanted no one to question or seek that which had been her father's.

"I thought the western isles. I have a cousin who serves a lord there and who would take us in until . . ."

"Until?" she asked. Though she could think again, she could not think clearly or too far into the future.

"Until it is safe and until you decide what you want to do."

"I know what I need to do, Godrod," she said, understanding that she must admit her guilt to the one most wronged by her actions. "We must go to Durness."

Gavin's descent into madness took little time at all. 'Twas as though his soul, at once understanding that he would not see Katla again, could no longer hold back the chaos and the clamor. Days after the ritual when the voices began their taunting, they soon took on the din of hundreds of horns blaring inside his head. After two months of relative peace, the pain roared back with such ferocity that he feared madness would be his only refuge.

Haakon began to feed him ale laced with some brew, something he'd used before Katla's calming effect, but it did no good. With weeks left until the next full moon, he foresaw only pain and suffering until he died during that last ritual. But none of that mattered, because his heart had broken at the loss of her. The pain in his head paled when compared to the one in his heart. He would be at some ease once he knew she was safe with Harald.

So he waited.

The moment Harald entered the chamber, Gavin knew something was terribly wrong. Worse, his deafness prevented him from hearing any explanation. Now all he could do was worry until he could hear again. He set Haakon to packing and sent word to King Edgar's steward that he was ready to leave. As a courtesy, and probably in the hopes of attracting Gavin to his court if his allegiance to Earl Magnus ever waned, Edgar offered them passage back to Orkney on a large, swift ship.

A terrible sense of foreboding filled Gavin as they sailed north and worse, the power seemed to build far in advance of the waxing moon. When someone touched his hand, he would hear bits and pieces of thoughts or memories from the person. If he concentrated, he could make it happen. Only in short bursts and not as clear as during the ritual, but it happened too many times on the voyage north for Gavin not to recognize that the power was approaching some precipice. Harald noticed it, but did not ask him about it. Haakon knew it, too.

On the fifth day of the journey, his hearing returned and he finally learned the details of Katla's disappearance. The only thing that consoled him was the knowledge that Godrod must be with her and that they had enough coins and gold to pay for food, supplies, and passage out of Scotland.

Once the voices began in earnest, he could think very little. By the time they arrived in Durness, he was back to the screaming madman he'd been when Katla had found him in the cave. So many voices, so many thoughts, so much pain.

The ale did not work. The wine did not work. The healer's brew did not work. So Gavin existed in pain, day and night, whether in the cave or out of it. He tried staying in the cottage above the cliffs, but every place in it reminded him of Katla and brought some memory of their time together back to him. Like the taunting in his mind, the memories mocked every hope he'd dared allow himself to have during those days. So he left, walking off into the hills, carrying only a skin of the drug-tinged ale with him for the small measure of relief it gave his body.

As though something else guided his feet, two days later Gavin stumbled into the circle of stones and fell there in the center. Exhausted, empty, and in pain, he could go no farther. Though he heard the same laughter there, he could not tell whether it was someone else's thoughts or produced by the strong herbs in his ale. And he did not care.

Haakon would follow and retrieve him when the earl's emissary arrived for the ritual. Until then it mattered not where he slept or if he did, for without Katla there was no peace.

It had taken weeks, but they'd crossed the land of the Scots and then hired a boat to take them north. Skirting along the western coast between Scotland and the isles now ruled by the Norse king, they made good time due to fair winds and unusually calm seas for this time of year.

The Gaels with whom they traveled shared stories to pass the time, and Katla learned much of the history of the places they saw along the way. And though they all worshipped the Christian God, some still spoke of the Old Ones and the coming festival of Samhain when the beings in the spirit world could cross into the physical one. Katla shivered when the old woman described the process to her, but something rang true in her words.

The end of the month approached when the second full moon would occur, and Katla wondered if Gavin would return to Durness for it. She thought he would. She would wait for him in Durness.

The waters churned dangerously and wildly, and the boat could go no farther, so she and Godrod decided to travel the final miles over land. They passed through an area called Assynt and through the hills of Quinag as they headed into the Southerlands and toward Durness. Finally, they entered a valley that looked and felt familiar to her.

The valley curved, and as they followed the stream running through it, Katla realized where their path would lead. As the sun drifted low in the sky and night was only a few hours away, they saw the ring of stones in the distance. Katla pushed on, something pulling her to that circle. She waved Godrod back when they reached it, entering alone.

This time, the whispers grew louder around her, and she turned this way and that, fooled by their strength and clarity into thinking others spoke to her. Katla walked toward the rise in the middle of the circle and would have tripped over him if she'd not been looking down at that moment.

Gavin lay senseless at her feet, unmoving and barely breathing.

Chapter Twenty-four

He opened his eyes and saw her once more.
His angel had returned, though he was certain it was too late to save him. Mayhap she would play the role of Valkyrie this night and guide his soul to the land of the dead?

It mattered not, for all his hopes were gone, all his dreams crushed, his life worthless. Death promised to be an easier path than life was now. He lifted his head and saw the moon rising and felt its pull in his blood.

He turned his head and gazed into eyes he knew, that gaze he'd never thought to see again. He breathed her name.

"Katla."

She remained standing above him, surrounded by the glittering stars as they made their appearance in the growing night sky above her. Her hair floated around her, reflecting the light of those stars, and he heard her voice, piercing through the tumult in his mind, for he heard it with his heart.

"Gavin," she said, and his heart raced at the sound.

His blood pounded through his veins, and he felt his body stir to life. Pushing himself up off the ground, he blinked to clear the dizziness away and looked around them. The circle filled with wisps of light that swirled around. But the touch of her hand on his face made everything else disappear.

"I . . ." she began.

He placed his finger on her mouth and shook his head. "No words," he pleaded. "I have too many in my head."

"No words then," she said, nodding in agreement with his request.

He'd had this dream before, and so he let it flow again, reaching out to touch her face and kiss her mouth. Not certain what was real and what was fantasy and blind hope, Gavin held her close, afraid she would disappear as quickly as she'd appeared before him. As he lifted his lips from the possessive joining of their mouths, Gavin began to hear her body.

The joy and sheer pleasure of those sounds pushed all others away, and his body responded to her nearness, to her touch, and to her scent. His heart sang in response to the music her body made as they undressed each other. The overwhelming desire that shot through him when he held her naked in his arms nearly took away his control. Then, something else took over, and he was carried away by it as he loved her, loved her for the last time.

Soon there was no beginning or end to either of them; their bodies and hearts merged in the passion that spun out around them and through them. They breathed as one, they moved as one, they felt pleasure as one. As they pursued that moment of satisfaction, of joining, of completion, Gavin knew he would always love her.

If only they had more time.

That thought flitted through his mind while their bodies exploded together and passion overwhelmed them. It was a long time before either one could move, and so they lay, still joined, still in the euphoria that such passion created, ignoring the force that would pull them apart. Katla was the first to speak, and he listened, still surprised that he heard only her voice and no other.

"I need to tell you something, Gavin," she began.

He sat up, shaking his head to stop her. The moon rose over the line of trees, and he could feel the power beginning to flow. There was little time and he wanted to tell her so much.

"Katla, there are things you must know," he said. "Things I could not tell you."

She stood then and stepped back. Reaching for her tunic, she pulled it on quickly. Godrod was out there somewhere and, just as before, she thought she saw someone walking outside the stone pillars.

"I lied to you, Gavin." She needed to tell him the truth about her actions. He needed to know. "I lied to gain your cooperation. I dragged you into my plot knowing you would suffer. I . . ." She stuttered then, unable to say the words.

"I know you lied." His words stopped her. "You have no knowledge of my past."

"You knew?" She frowned at him. "Then why did you agree to help me?"

"I am the Truthsayer, it is my task to hear the truth."

She sensed that he was still avoiding the complete truth. She could hear it in his voice. She could feel it in her heart. "Why did you help me?"

"Because you have given me so much, I wanted to repay you."

"I gave you pain. I gave you lies. I kidnapped you, Gavin."

He smiled, and the sadness of his look touched her heart. "You gave me moments of peace and silence such as I'd never felt before. You gave me moments of hope that let me see a possible future for myself. You gave me yourself time and time again to ease my pain, even when you had every reason not to." He laughed then. "Even now when you should hate me for speaking the words that damned your father and your brother, you feel pain for me."

Tears gathered in her eyes and spilled over her cheeks at his words. She'd thought he'd only sought the pleasures of the flesh from her. She'd thought only her body was of interest for the passion he could stir within her and the satisfaction he could find with her. But it was the emotions created by their joining that he treasured.

"I wish I could give you what you need most, Gavin. Godrod will search out more knowledge and we will find . . ."

"There is no time, Katla," he said, his voice changing as it always did for the truthspeaking. "This will be my last ritual."

She looked around, searching for the person who would hear the truth and saw no one. "Your last ritual? I do not understand. Who, Gavin? Whose truth will you speak?"

His eyes changed next, glowing from within and losing all the color until only light shone forth. His face seemed to melt, and another's took its place. When he grabbed her hand and she felt power surge into her body and her mind, she understood.

"I hear your truth, Katla Svensdottir," the voice said.

He pulled her forward into some place that she'd never seen before. Even though their bodies did not move, their minds seemed to travel through the air around them. Lights flickered around them, and so many voices surrounded them that she felt dizzy.

"I hear your truth, Katla." Gavin's voice spoke alone in her thoughts. "Too many other voices have told part of it, though none have told it all. Hear it now," he ordered, and she could do nothing but listen as voices shouted out at her from all sides.

Her father's anger at the earl. Her uncle goading him to take action. Her brother pleading with her father to give him a role. Gavin speaking of his love for her. Harald offering a place in his household and more. It went on and on and on until she thought she would scream. Every aspect of her had taken on a voice, and the manipulations of all the players had been exposed by the Truthsayer's abilities.

The last thing she heard was Gavin telling of his coming death. She screamed then, not wanting to hear of it and not wanting it to happen before she admitted her true feelings to him.

"I lied," she called out, though she was uncertain he could hear. "I lied to you, Gavin. Hear me!"

Suddenly he was gone from her mind, from her thoughts, and she was alone with so many facts now known. She felt his hand slip from hers and opened her eyes to see him sinking to his knees before her. His face became his own, and his voice returned.

"You lied to me, Katla," he whispered, and then he collapsed at her feet.

She knelt down and called out for Godrod. Leaning Gavin back, she placed her hand on his chest and felt his heart slowing under her palm.

"No! Gavin!" she yelled, and she shook him. "You cannot die now." She screamed as his chest stopped drawing breath. "Gavin!" His sightless eyes stared back at her. She clutched him to her and whispered against his skin. " 'Twas not only a bargain, Gavin. I lied when I said that. It was more than that between us." She cried, tears pouring down her face, knowing he would never hear the one thing, the most important thing she needed to say to him now.

But she said it anyway.

Leaning close to his ear, she whispered the words no one had ever said to him. The thing he needed most. The thing she had not realized until she'd heard the truth he spoke to her.

"I love you, Gavin. I love you."

Silence reigned around them; nothing moved; no one spoke. Only Katla's sobbing breaths broke into it and echoed across the circle. So, when it happened, it was loud enough for both Katla and Godrod to hear.

An indrawn breath. And then another. Then Gavin's heart began to beat once more under her hand. Katla looked at his face and he stared back.

Alive! He lived!

She touched his face and his skin, and he was alive. Gavin lifted his hand and touched her face, wiping away some of her tears with his thumb. He slid his hand into her hair and pulled her face to his, kissing her mouth and whispering words against it.

"I love you, Katla Svensdottir. I will always love you."

She kissed him back with all the love she had within her, all the love she'd denied feeling for him. Then she helped him to his feet.

"Can you hear me, Gavin?"

"Aye, love. I hear you, though I do not understand how. My ears do not burn and there is no pain." He paused for a moment and then laughed out loud. "And no thoughts, either!"

"How? How can this be?" she asked as Godrod handed Gavin his tunic and he dressed quickly.

Before either of them could offer any ideas, sounds began around them. First laughter like the tinkling of bells filled the air. Then whispers from near the stones. Katla watched as figures moved in the shadows. Clutching Gavin's hand and afraid to let him go, she nodded as one figure, a man, separated himself from the circle and approached them.

Unlike any man she'd ever seen, this one was too beautiful to look on for long. He looked regal, wearing the long robes of nobles, his face pale yet lit with some strength from within. His gaze met hers first, and she realized that his eyes were the same as Gavin's—during the ritual! Every step he took toward them echoed through the circle, and when he stopped before them and smiled, lights glimmered around them like fireflies of every color. Katla stared at his face and recognized it, too, for it was the face that Gavin took on during that time.

Was this the creature, the being, who took Gavin over, the one responsible for the power he had?

"Who are you?" Gavin asked, pulling her close to his side and away from the man.

"We are Sith," he answered in a voice that was filled with many and sounded like music in the air around them. "You are Sith," he said to Gavin.

Gavin shook his head in denial. "It cannot be." Gavin looked at her and repeated, "It cannot be."

The being laughed and the stars above flared brightly. He approached them and reached out his hand. Katla cringed, but he laughed again in that magical voice. "Fear not, human. Our touch harms you not." The Sith placed his hand on theirs and whispered without his mouth moving.

"Hear your truth, Truthsayer." Katla heard it as well, shocked again by the power that surged through her from just the touch of the Sith's hand and Gavin's. "Learn how you came to be."

The words flowed into her mind, and then a vision was revealed there in the circle.

"Many years ago as humans count time, I discovered a woman in the western isles. Her beauty drew me and I came to her in the day and the night, giving her my love."

Gavin realized that this Sith told the story as a human would, now referring to only himself alone. He watched with Katla as a young woman appeared in the circle near them, beautiful and filled with life.

"I took her to my lands through an entrance like that one," the Sith said, nodding at the rise in the center of the stones, "and we spent many months there together. I gave her everything," he said fiercely, "but she was not happy and asked to return to her mortal world and the man she'd been betrothed to before I found her. She refused my love and found her way back here on a Samhain night twenty-and-eight years ago as you count time."

The Sith turned from them then and nodded at the place before them, and Gavin saw it as it had happened. He thought only he was seeing the vision until he heard Katla's gasp and felt her hold tightly on to his hand.

The young woman appeared again, this time pushing her way out of the fairy hill. She was huge with child as she stumbled out of the ground, holding her belly and moaning against the pain of impending birth. She kept looking behind her to see if anyone followed, and then she began to run toward the path.

But she did not make it, falling to the ground as her pains struck. When she looked over her shoulder before gaining her feet once more, the Sith stood there on the fairy hill.

"Do not leave," he said. "I gave you my love." Gavin had not supposed this creature capable of such mortal emotions. But his love and pain were clear as the Sith spoke.

"Come back with me now." He held out his hand to her but she turned away, trying to run.

"I cannot live with you. I do not love you," she said, gasping for breath as another pain struck. She howled in pain but still turned away. "Let me go!" she screamed.

The Sith's rage and pain exploded then. Flashes of light and waves of heat pierced the night sky as he lashed out at the woman who'd betrayed him. Katla shook at Gavin's side.

"They are mine," he said, pointing at her huge belly. "They are gifted." Something flashed from his hand to the woman's belly, and she screamed in pain. "But they will be cursed for your betrayal. When they use their Sith powers, their mortal lives will suffer. Their powers will grow and their mortal bodies will suffer. When their powers peak and end, they will wither and die."

"No!" she screamed. "Please! Do not make my bairns carry the punishment for my sins against you," she cried out, pulling herself up onto her knees and reaching out her hand to him. "Spare them, I beg you!"

The Sith approached her and crouched down in front of her then, placing his hand on her belly for only a moment. Gavin stared at the scene and watched some indescribable emotion fill the Sith's face as he felt the bairns inside her womb.

"They will be taken from you, for you are not worthy to raise them. They will not know of their powers or the source of it, and you cannot tell them or the Sith will strike you all down," he commanded.

She began to crawl away as though to escape his sentence, but he shook his head at her and waved his hand. Four others appeared around her, holding her and keeping her from running.

"Unless they find true love, given and spoken by one called enemy or betrayer, their Sith nature will destroy their human one and they will live in our world forever. If they find that true love, given and spoken, before their powers end, their mortal nature will control their Sith side."

Gavin could not move as the story explaining his life unfolded before them, like a vision. The scene sped up, and Katla grasped his hand as they watched the woman give birth to three bairns, all boys. As each was born, one of the other Sith took the babe and disappeared. When the birth was complete, the last Sith faded away, leaving only the woman and the first Sith alone.

The Sith shook his head at her. "You will not find what you seek with him. You will suffer this loss and more by refusing what I offered you. Only one of the three can help you find the happiness you seek."

"No," the woman keened out. "No more!"

"I do not curse you, Aigneis," he said softly now. "I only see what the failure of your mortal heart will cause."

Gavin could not speak as he watched the Sith walk to the fairy hill and fade into it. The vision of that Samhain night faded, too, until it was the present day and the moon shone high in the night sky overhead. Katla wiped her face and turned to him. Finally they understood the power that had controlled his life and the reasons behind it.

The Sith's eyes glowed as he turned to face them once more. "That was your past, born of betrayal, half Sith, half mortal. Destined only to survive in this mortal world if you could find the one thing that I could not."

"And my mother? Does she yet live?" Gavin asked him.

The Sith, his father, smiled then. "She lives."

"My brothers?" He turned to Katla and smiled. "I have brothers," he said. The sadness in her eyes was fleeting, soon replaced by happiness for him. "Where are they?"

"I cannot tell you that. They face their own challenges, just as you did."

"Can I find them?" he asked.

"Your powers are just beginning," he explained, calling Gavin by another name then, one that floated in the air around them. "You can find them with her help." The Sith glanced at Katla then and smiled.

"My help?" Katla shook her head. "I have no powers."

"Ah, but you have the most potent of powers within you. You saved his life with it."

Gavin understood. "Your love for me, Katla. I heard you calling me back from the darkness when my heart stopped."

The Sith's gaze softened then as he smiled. " 'Twas a piece of your heart and soul left behind in him that saved his mortal life this day. Your love, given over these last months and then spoken today, freed him from the curse laid on him in anger."

The Sith moved away from them then, walking and floating toward the small hill where the entrance to his land was, but he stopped and stared back at them.

"I would see my son's son when he is born."

Confused by the words, Gavin frowned. "What do you mean?"

The Sith floated back to Katla and reached out, touching only a finger on her belly. She startled, and then her face filled with a glow of her own.

"She carries your son in her womb. He is gifted."

Gavin lost his breath with those words. His eyes filled with tears as so many dreams and hopes spread out before him. Instead of meeting his end this night, he'd received the chance to live his dream with the woman he loved.

"Summon me when he is born," the Sith said only to him, speaking in his thoughts as he revealed the name he was called. Then before either could say a thing, the Sith faded until only the stars sparkled above them.

Gavin grabbed Katla and held her tightly, swinging her around him in a circle again and again until she screamed. They laughed for a long time, in joy, in surprise, and in love. He still could not believe what had happened, but he finally knew how he had come to be and what his future held.

Now he wanted to live and love as any other man did, cherishing the woman at his side. Godrod stepped back, giving them privacy to share this moment.

"You lied about something else, Katla," he said, kissing her mouth. "When we joined in the truthspeaking, I heard a story told about the Old Ones and about standing stones in the west of Scotland. You did learn something of my origins, just not enough to understand."

"Do you think we can find your brothers? Find out if they survived the curse of their gift as you did?"

Gavin thought on the other things the Sith told him in his

thoughts, things Katla had not heard. "I know a way," he said. "But we must try it before the moon sets."

"Here?" she asked. "Now?"

"My powers are strongest on the anniversary of my birth and during the full moon," he explained, repeating what the Sith had told him silently.

"'Tis that night and the moon is yet full. . . ." Her words faded off and she nodded.

Soon the sound of their passion filled the circle, and if it took several times to learn how to control his power and to send it out in search of his brothers, neither complained.

Epilogue

Oidhche Shamhna (Samhain Night)
One year later

During the months after that fateful night, the Truthsayer disappeared and the man lived. Haakon sent news of Gavin's death to Harald and the earl and emptied everything that had been Gavin's out of the cave and the cottage. Though she'd used much of the money gained by selling her jewelry, Katla had more than enough to support them for many, many years.

They changed their names and moved south, searching for Gavin's brothers. The clue she had linking the stone circles to the Sith led them to more knowledge, though most of it was in folktales and the wisdom of the elders of clans and families along the coast. With each full moon, Gavin sent out his power, listening for any sign of his brothers. He had no success, but they both hoped that the anniversary of his birth would prove an auspicious day for him.

The bairn, a boy as the Sith had declared, was born at the beginning of August, and they called him Callum in the fashion of the Gaels because his grandmother came from there.

One night after his birth, Gavin summoned his father, using the name that had power over him. Katla held the babe, fearful of handing him over to such a being, but Gavin assured her no harm would come to their son.

The Sith had touched his head to the babe's and sniffed. "Human and Sith, he will be called . . ."

Whatever the name was, she could not comprehend or repeat it, but Gavin did. The strangest thing was the way the babe smiled at his grandfather and father as though he understood the name, too. Katla suspected this would be the first of many things that would be between father and son because of the Sith nature they shared.

Now though, the night approached and Katla had left the babe at their farm with the servant who cared for him while she accompanied Gavin into the woods. They'd discovered not a circle of stones but a few ancient markers left behind about a mile from their farm. Gavin tugged her along, and they arrived just as the moon rose. Not a full moon this year, but Samhain night still held a certain magic for him.

He spread his cloak on the ground for them, but when he began to kiss her beside the largest of the stones, they forgot all about it. Gavin lifted her in his arms and guided her down on his erect cock. Leaning her back against the stone's surface, he thrust deeply into her flesh, rocking in and out until she felt the rippling spasms begin at her core. She kissed him just before the release was upon her and urged him to hurry.

As his seed began to spill, the power surged through both of them, lifting them from their place and letting them soar in the air above. Night became day as they journeyed along the coast of Scotland. Gavin leaned his head back and listened for a familiar voice, seeking it and following it south to the glen of Kilmartin, where they saw a man who looked much like Gavin. He called out his name to them as they passed.

"Connor!" they said together.

Gavin pulled her along, and Katla laughed at the feeling of such freedom and the sight of the land from above like this. She did not know how it happened, but she trusted Gavin to keep her safe. They moved farther west, across the water, until they reached the large isle of Skye. The view of it became hazy then, but a castle sat above the shoreline and there, on the battlements, stood his other brother.

"Duncan!" they called out together, watching as he faded into the mist of the power.

They came back into themselves in that moment, and Katla felt the last spasms of her release and his within her. Gavin smiled then and laughed. "I know where they are!" He kissed her again and again and the joy and love spread through them.

Soon they did use that cloak, and by the time the sun rose in the morning sky, their pleasure and love surrounded them like a storm, keeping them safe and becoming stronger with each moment.

Kilmartin Glen, southwestern Scotland
Oidhche Shamhna (Samhain Night)

Connor awoke with a start in the middle of the night. After the hours he'd spent making love with Moira, he should be sleeping as soundly as she was. But something, someone, had interrupted his rest by calling out his name. Just as he was sinking back into sleep's grasp, he heard it again.

And he knew what it meant and who called to him using the power they'd inherited from their Sith father. Smiling, he shook Moira gently, knowing she would be furious if he knew and did not share the knowledge with her.

"Connor, is something wrong?" she asked, turning into his embrace in their bed. Even waking from a sound sleep, her voice lured him into passion. Would he ever tire of her?

"I heard him again, Moira." He kissed her head and held her tightly at his side. "My brother."

She awoke then, pushing herself up to sit. "Your brother? Truly? Could you tell which one?"

"Aye, the one called Gavin. He searches for me and for Duncan even now."

"So he lives?" She kissed him and smiled. "Can you guide him to us? Or us to him?"

Before he could speak, her hand encircled his cock and he choked. " 'Tis still Samhain and you know about your powers on Samhain night, Connor."

He would love her until he died and probably even beyond that, for her love and her enthusiasm never waned.

"Aye, wife, I know about my powers." He guided her hand into a pleasing rhythm, and then he reached over to touch between her legs, feeling the arousal of her body and the heat awaiting him there. She slid down next to him then, the sounds of her pleasure warming his blood.

"Call forth your visions, Seer," she commanded using the name his father had called him, the name she had learned. "Call forth your visions."

Samhain proved his powers once again, and in the morning, he knew where to find Gavin.

The cave where Gavin lived, called Smûga by the Norse, is found on the northwest coast of Scotland in the area known as Sutherland. It is partially a sea cave and a karst cave, carved into the cliffs by the action of the waves and a river that eroded holes into the limestone over eons. There is archaeological evidence from a variety of time periods showing that humans have lived in it. Viking artifacts have been uncovered, too.

I found Smoo Cave by accident while researching for this story. As I wrote the ending of *A Storm of Passion*, I learned that the second brother lived by the sea, in a large cave that opened to the north toward Orkney. In trying to find if such a location existed, I found references to Smoo Cave, and while in Scotland in 2009, I was able to visit the cave. It is wildly fascinating—huge, made of many chambers, with a waterfall and river running through it to the sea. And when I stood between the crashing waterfall and the opening of the cave to the sea, I could hear very little except the rushing water.

It was perfect! There were chambers of different sizes that went back into the limestone—some damp and cold, some dryer but still cold! There were "blowholes" in the ceiling, open to the ground above. It was exactly as I'd seen in my mind as the place where Gavin seeks refuge, so I took lots of photos and used them to describe the cave in this story. I just love it when real history works out the way I want and need it to for my stories!

The ring of standing stones that I describe in this story as being near Durness is of my own making, though Scotland

and its northern and western isles are rife with circles and henges and burial cairns and chambered tombs . . . and filled with places that echo back to a time when *sith* or *fae* magic still glimmered in the highlands and islands. And the strange, eerie feeling of being watched that crept down my spine as I walked the stones at Callanish and Brodgar and Stenness, and explored the burial chambers at Maes Howe, Mine Howe, and the Tomb of the Eagles told me that there is much, much more about these places than we will ever know.

I have adapted some of the real history of the times and places and adjusted some historical events and people (like shifting the reigns of Earl, later Saint, Magnus and the Norse King Magnus Barelegs) to fit my story. I beg the indulgence of anyone who notices such things.

Please visit my website (www.terribrisbin.com) to see some photos I took on my 2009 trip to Scotland, including Smoo Cave, Orkney, Skye, and Mull. Happy Reading!

Everyone likes to be on THE NAUGHTY LIST now and again. Don't miss this sexy anthology featuring Donna Kauffman, Cynthia Eden, and Susan Fox, out now. Here's a sneak peek of Donna's story, "Naughty but Nice."

Griff's train of thought was abruptly broken by a loud yelp coming from somewhere in the rear of the small shop, followed by a ringing crash of what sounded like metal on metal.

He gritted his teeth against the renewed ringing inside his own head, even as he called out in the ensuing silence. "Hullo? Are you in need of some assistance?"

What followed was a stream of very . . . colorful language that surprised a quick smile from him. He'd found Americans, at least the ones of his immediate acquaintance, to be a bit obsessed with political correctness, always worrying what others might think. So it was somewhat refreshing, to hear such an . . . uncensored reaction. He assumed the string of epithets wasn't a response to his query, but then he'd never met the proprietor.

He debated heading around the counter to see if she might need help, then checked the action. "No need to engage an angry female unless absolutely necessary," he murmured, tipping up onto his toes and looking behind the counter, on the off chance he might spy the pot of coffee. "Ah," he said, on seeing a double burner positioned beside an empty, tiered glass case.

He fished out his wallet and put a ten note on the counter, more than enough to cover the cost of a single cup, then ducked under the counter and scanned the surface for a stack of insulated cups. Oversized, sky blue mugs with the shop's white and pink cupcake logo printed on one side and the name on the other, were lined up next to the machine. He didn't think she'd take too kindly to his leaving with one of those.

"Making an angry female even angrier . . . never a good thing." His mouth lifted again as a few more, rather unique invectives floated from the back of the shop. "Points for creativity, however."

He glanced at his watch, saw he still had some time, and took a moment to roll his neck, shake out his shoulders, and relax his jaw. He could feel the tension tightening him up, which was a fairly common state of late. But he'd never been so close to realizing his every dream. He fished out the small airline-sized tube of pain relievers he'd bought when he'd landed. Upon popping it open, he discovered there was only one tablet left. He shrugged and dry swallowed it.

He crouched down to look under the counter and had just opened a pair of cupboard doors when he felt a presence behind him.

"May I help you with something?"

Hmm. Angry female, immediately south of his wide open back. He was fairly certain there were sharp knives within reach. Not the best strategy he'd ever employed.

Already damned, he reached inside the cupboard and slid a large insulated cup from the stack, snagging a plastic lid as well, before gently closing the doors and straightening up. "Just looking for a cup," he said as he turned, a careful smile on his face.

The smile froze as he got his first look at the cupcake baker. He wasn't normally taken to poetic thought, but there he stood, thinking her clear, almost luminescent skin made her wide, dark blue eyes look like twin pools of endlessly deep, midnight waters. It was surprisingly difficult to keep from looking away, every self-protective instinct he had being triggered by her steady hold on his gaze, which was rather odd. She was the village baker. Despite the tirade he'd just overheard, he doubted anyone who made baking cheerful little cakes her life's work would be a threat or obstacle to his mission. "I hope you don't mind," he said, lifting the cup so she could see what he'd been about. "You sounded a bit . . . occupied, back there."

"Yes, a little problem with a collapsed rolling rack."

His gaze, held captive as it was, used the time to quickly take in the rest of her. Thick, curling hair almost the same rich brown as the steaming hot brew he'd yet to sip had been pulled up in an untidy knot on the back of her head, exposing a slender length of neck, and accentuating her delicate chin. All of which combined to showcase a pair of unpainted, full, dark pink lips that, even when not smiling, curved oh-so-naturally into the kind of perfect bow that all but begged a man to part them, taste them, bite them, and . . .

He looked away. Damn. He couldn't recall his body ever leaping to attention like that, after a single look. No matter how direct. Especially when his attentions were clearly not being encouraged in any way, if the firm set of her delicate chin was any indication.

"Nothing too serious, I hope," he said, boldly turning his back to her and helping himself to a cup of coffee. After all, he'd paid for it. Not that she was aware of it as yet. But he thought it better to risk her mild displeasure until he could point that out . . . rather than engage more of the fury he'd heard coming from the back of the shop minutes ago—which he was fairly certain would be the case if her sharp gaze took in the current state of the front of his trousers.

"Nothing another five hours of baking time won't resolve," she said, a bit of weariness creeping into her tone. From the corner of his eye, he caught her wiping her hands on the flour covered front of her starched white baker's jacket. "Please, allow me."

He quickly topped off the cup and snapped on the lid. "Not to worry. I believe I've got it. I left a ten note on your counter."

"I'm sorry," she said, sounding sincere. "It's been . . . a morning. I'm generally not so—"

"It's fine," he said, intending to skirt past her and duck back to the relative safety of the other side of the counter. The tall, trouser-concealing counter. He just needed a moment, preferably with her not in touching distance, so he could button his coat and allow himself a bit of recovery time. It seemed all he had to do was look at her for his current state to remain . . . elevated.

Unfortunately for him, and the comfort level of his trousers, she moved closer and reached past him. "The sugar is here and I have fresh cream in the—"

"I take it black," he said abruptly, then they both turned the same way, trapping her between the counter . . . and him.

Her gaze honed in on his once again, but he was the one holding hers captive.

"Okay," she said, her voice no longer strident. In fact, the single word had been a wee bit . . . breathy.

"Indeed," he murmured, once again caught up in that mouth of hers. Those parted lips simply demanded a man pay them far more focused attention. *Step away, Gallagher,* he counseled himself. *Sip your coffee, gather your wits, and move on.*

Hungry for the holidays? Go out and get
THE BITE BEFORE CHRISTMAS,
Heidi Betts's first book for Brava, available now . . .

Connor's level of confidence where his younger siblings were concerned was quite a bit lower than his declaration made it sound.

Did he wish he had the power to influence Liam and Maeve's attitudes and actions? Certainly.

Had he had any success in doing so thus far? Not even remotely. And nothing that had happened in recent memory made him think he ever would.

But sitting across from the lovely Jillian Parker—the events planner Angelina had sent to help keep his holiday from becoming a complete and abysmal failure—he suddenly felt the need to preen . . . or at least to act as though being the patriarch of his family carried *some* weight with his unruly brother and sister.

Angelina had told him Jillian was good at what she did. His longtime friend had apparently attended several events that Jillian's company had organized, and had been quite impressed.

What Angelina *hadn't* told him was that Jillian Parker was *hot* with a capital *H* and two *T*s.

From the moment Randall had opened the door and invited her in . . . from the moment he'd stepped out of the library and sniffed the air, he'd known she wouldn't be just another random woman drifting in and out of his life. She smelled of peaches and cream and just hint of honey, all of which seeped into his pores and set his blood on fire.

It had been all he could do to walk calmly across the foyer to introduce himself. To take her hand instead of her mouth.

He *hadn't* been able to resist slipping his middle and index fingers over the inside of her wrist, however, to feel her pulse. To feel the beat of her heart in the one, slim vein, and the heat of her life's blood that called to his own.

Having her here, working in his home, was going to be an experience, that was for sure. And an exercise in self-control; something he'd always prided himself on . . . but now couldn't be entirely certain of.

Her blond hair was swept up in a loose knot at the back of her head, a few wisps falling free to frame her heart-shaped face and dust the pulse at her neck. He could see the gentle throb on both sides, even with the short distance that separated them.

She had bright blue eyes surrounded by light lashes and a raspberry-tinted mouth that could only be described as infinitely kissable.

Since it was winter in Boston, she was dressed more warmly and demurely than he suspected was the norm. Charcoal slacks and a thick red sweater with a deep, wide cowl neckline covered her from shoulder to ankle, but he could very well imagine the luscious figure hidden beneath.

Professional on the outside, sexy as hell on the inside. A flush of intense arousal heated his skin at the thought, moving south at a rapid pace.

Even in stylish boots with a two-inch heel, the top of her head only reached his chin while standing. But though petite, her form was lush and curvaceous, and made him feel both protective and possessive. Unusual given their short acquaintance, but not something Connor was inclined to question at the moment.

Clicking the tip of her pen, Jillian crossed her legs and adjusted the pad on her lap, ready to take notes.

"*That* I can do," she murmured, oblivious to the fact that he was nearly chewing nails on the other side of the desk, his mind having wandered hell and gone from worries about an ideal holiday celebration to stripping her of that soft sweater and exploring every inch of her soft, white skin.

Thankfully, the wide desk hid the proof of his distraction, but if he didn't drag this out for a while, she and everyone he came in contact with in the next little while would know exactly what he was thinking of doing to his attractive new party planner.

"So tell me what it is you're looking for in a holiday event. What would make your Christmas flawless with a capital *F?*"

Exhaling a deep breath, he rocked back and forth slightly in his cushioned black leather executive chair and did his best not to picture *her* beneath the tree on Christmas morning—naked and waiting for something that definitely started with a big, hard capitol F. And it wasn't *flawless.*

And be sure to look for
A DARKER SHADE OF DEAD
by Bianca D'Arc, coming next month!

"This blows."

Dr. Sandra McCormick's voice echoed around the morgue. Well, it wasn't really a morgue. At least it hadn't been. The large room had been a perfectly good laboratory until the senior team members had decided to perform tests on cadavers. Now it was a morgue.

The temperature had been dropped to near freezing and Sandra shivered in her lab coat. She'd donned her heaviest jacket under the lab coat she had borrowed from one of the men on the team who wore a much larger size, but it still wasn't enough. She was cold, dammit.

Cold and miserable and all alone on night shift because she was low man on the totem pole. The science team had been together for a few months, working for the military on ways to improve combat performance. Specifically, they'd been trying to come up with substances that, when injected into people, would improve healing and endurance in living tissue. They were at the point now where they'd graduated from *in vitro* testing in Petri dishes to something a bit more exotic.

They weren't ready to try *in vivo* testing on living animals or people. Instead, the senior scientists had decided to take this grotesque step, administering the experimental regenerative serum to dead tissue contained in a whole, deceased organism. Personally, she would've preferred to start with a dead animal of some kind, but only human cadavers would work for this experiment since the genetic manipulation they were attempting was coded specifically for human tissue. They didn't want any cross-contamination with animals if they found a substance that actually worked.

As a result, she was stuck in a freezing cold lab in the middle of the night, watching a bunch of dead Marines. It was kind of sad, actually. Every one of these men had been cut down in their prime by either illness or injury. They had all been highly trained and honed specimens of manhood while they were alive. Some of them had been quite handsome, but their beauty had been lost to the pale coldness of death. They were here because they had no next of kin—only their beloved Corps—and their bodies had been donated to science.

The room was dimly lit. Sandra only needed the individual lights over each metal table on which the bodies rested to do her work. She'd holed up at a desk in the far corner of the giant lab space, entering the data she collected hourly for each body into a computer. Her fingers were already numb from the cold and it had only been three hours. Five more to go before the day shift would release her from this icy prison.

She heard a rustling sound in the distance as she blew on her fingers to try to warm them up. Her chair swiveled as she lifted her feet, placing them on the runners of the rolling office chair.

"That better not have been the sound of mice scampering around in here."

Contrary to most medical researchers, Sandra had never really been comfortable with mice. Little furry rodents still made her jump and she shied away from any lab work that required her to deal with the critters.

The room was dimly lit. The only illumination came from the computer screen and desk light behind her and the single light over each table. The whole setup gave her the creeps.

Deciding to brave the walk to the bank of light switches on the far side of the room near the door, Sandra stood. If she had to sit here with a bunch of dead bodies all night, the least she could do was put on every light in the damned room. Why she'd ever thought the desk light would be enough, she didn't know.

She'd gone on shift at midnight and was slated to take readings every hour until 8 a.m. when her day shift counterpart would relieve her. Scientific work sometimes required a person to work odd hours. Experiments didn't know how to tell time. When they were running something in the lab, she usually got tapped for the late night hours. Normally she didn't mind. The lab was usually a peaceful, comforting place.

But not now. Not when it had been turned into a morgue. Or maybe it was more like Dr. Frankenstein's dungeon, only without the bug eyed servant named Igor. She'd definitely seen that old Mel Brooks movie one too many times in college. Thinking about some of the funnier lines from the comedy classic made her smile as she walked down the aisle of tables toward the door and the light switches.

"It's alive . . ." She did a quiet imitatiion of Gene Wilder from the scene where he'd given life to his monster as she walked, chuckling to herself.

One either side of her were slabs on which the cadavers rested. A breeze ruffled one of the sheets that had been pulled over the body on her right.

It must've been a breeze. The sheet couldn't move on its own, right? She quickened her step, a creepy feeling shivering down her spine as the smile left her face.

A hand shot out of the dark and grabbed her wrist. She screamed. The fingers were cold. The flesh was gray. But the grip was strong. Too strong.

It pulled her in. Closer and closer to the body she'd checked only forty-five minutes before. He'd been dead at the time. Immobile. Now he was moving and—oh, God—his eyes were open and he was looking at her. His stare was lifeless as he drew her closer.

She did her best to break free but the dead man was just too strong. She beat against his fingers with her other hand. When that didn't work, she tried pushing against his cold shoulder. Nothing seemed to help. She hit his face, his chest, anyplace she could reach, but he wouldn't let go.

He drew her closer until she was leaning across him, her arm over his head. Then he opened his mouth . . . and bit her. She gasped as his teeth broke through her skin. Blood welled as the icy teeth sank deep. Dull eyes looked through her as the dead man chewed on her forearm.

She went crazy, struggling to break free. She must've twisted in the right way because after a moment, she felt herself moving more easily. The next second, she was free.

He sat up, following her progress. She heard noises all around the lab now, echoing off the shadowed walls. She looked around in a panic. Other bodies were rising all around the makeshift morgue.

"How in God's name . . . ?" She gasped, clutching her bleeding arm to her chest as six tall bodies slid off the laboratory tables to stand in the dim, chilled room. She was so scared, she nearly wet her pants. The fear gave her a spike of clarity. She had to get out of there.

She ran for the door. Hands grabbed at her lab coat. She stumbled but caught herself before she could fall to the cold floor. She let her arms slip backward so the oversized lab coat came off, held in those strong hands that had come at her out of the darkness. She had no idea what had gone wrong with the experiment but she wasn't about to stick around to ask questions. These guys were huge. Big Marines who were easily twice her size. And they didn't seem friendly. In fact, they kept grabbing at her.

If she could just get to the door. She ran, dodging and weaving around the tables and the reaching arms. They tried to grab the jacket she'd worn under the oversized lab coat, but they had a hard time getting hold of the slippery nylon fabric, thank goodness.

She crashed through the door, running for her life. She had to get help. She had to rouse the entire team. She had to get the MPs and the Marines and hell, the National Guard if she could, to stop these guys.

She turned to look over her shoulder just once as she ran into the fringe of trees on the heavily wooded outskirts of the base. What she saw chilled her to the bone. In the dark of the night, she could see the dim, yellow, rectangular glow of the open doorway. Outlined there were the hulking shapes of dead men. The dead Marines were following her path outdoors at a slow, steady, lurching pace.